CH

THE RIGHT MR WRONG

When Tiphanie tells her boyfriend Howard she'll have to cancel their holiday to go and help her brother look after their niece and nephew, the consequences are catastrophic. Reeling from the break-up, Tiphanie arrives at her brother's home in a beautiful area close to the salt marshes, anticipating just a little peace and quiet. But any such hopes are dashed thanks to inconvenient feline escapades, a couple of very lively children, and her rather irksome — yet gorgeous — neighbour Kyle . . .

Books by Pat Posner
in the Linford Romance Library:

PRESCRIPTION FOR HAPPINESS
SUNLIGHT ON SHADOWS
TANGLED WEB
ROMANCE IN THE AIR
A SONG ON THE JUKEBOX
A SURPRISE ENGAGEMENT

PAT POSNER

THE RIGHT
MR WRONG

Complete and Unabridged

LINFORD
Leicester

First published in Great Britain in 2017

First Linford Edition
published 2018

A catalogue record for this book is available
from the British Library.

ISBN 978–1–4448–3813–8

Published by
F. A. Thorpe (Publishing)
Anstey, Leicestershire

Set by Words & Graphics Ltd.
Anstey, Leicestershire
Printed and bound in Great Britain by
T. J. International Ltd., Padstow, Cornwall

This book is printed on acid-free paper

1

'I must have been out of my mind when I agreed to do this,' said Tiphanie as she lifted the holdalls out of the car boot and passed two to her friend.

'You said exactly the same thing before you did that spot on local radio,' Felicity reminded her. 'Look what happened then. You met Howard, and you've been an item for almost two months.'

Tiphanie nodded. 'And it was great when we discovered we'd both been booked for this festival, way back in time before we knew of each other's existence.'

'You'd have met here even if you hadn't both been on that programme. Fate meant for you to meet.'

Tiphanie closed the boot with a thud and pressed the remote to lock the car. 'It's OK for Howard.' She returned to

1

her earlier worry as they started to walk across the country hotel's parking area. 'He's used to running workshops. And *Brawn and Bedlington* is such a popular sitcom, everybody has heard of it. Which is why he was booked for the entire festival and I was only asked for the second week.

'I bet half those who attend my workshops — that's if anyone does attend — won't even have seen my cartoon strips. They'll probably be expecting something like *Tintin* or *Peanuts* or *Pluggers*.'

'Never heard of *Pluggers*.' Felicity giggled.

'Whatever, they'll be expecting something entirely different from me and my *Fenland Frolics*. I'm really dreading the first workshop.'

'I don't feel so cool myself,' said Felicity. 'And I'll be hidden away in the kitchens. Not on show like you.'

'Fliss, you're not supposed to say things like that. You're here to boost my morale as well as creating delicious food.' Tiphanie's slow walk dwindled to almost a stop as she turned to glare at her best friend.

'OK.' Felicity grinned, then dropped her two holdalls and mimed ringing a hand-bell. 'Oyez! Oyez! Make way for Tiphanie Timpson, aka Tizzy, the almost-famous cartoonist; and her hilarious cartoon family, the *Fenland Frolics*! Don't miss out! Sign up for her workshops at the Lanleigh Writers' and Artists' Festival, now!'

'Idiot,' said Tiphanie, half-annoyed and half-amused at Felicity's antics. She took a quick look round, hoping there'd been nobody to see or hear. But they'd arrived early, and outside at least it was deserted.

Howard would be inside somewhere, though. Tiphanie suddenly realised how much she'd missed him during the last seven days. The fact she had something to tell him — something he would most definitely not like — only slightly overshadowed her eagerness to see him.

'Come on, Felicity.' She waved a

hand in the direction of a double-storey building separated from the hotel by a large cobbled courtyard. 'That must be the Conference Centre over there. Howard said it was a converted stable block.'

'Shame we're not staying in the hotel itself.' Felicity gave the elegant Georgian manor an admiring glance as they walked past it.

'Staying in a converted stable will be more fun,' stated Tiphanie. 'Especially as you'll be in charge of the catering team.'

'I just hope I'm up to it, Tizz.'

'Of course you are. You've catered for much bigger events than this. That's why I told you to get in touch with the organisers when Howard told me they hadn't got anyone to head up the catering staff for this week.'

'Yeah, well; thank you, I think,' said Felicity. 'Anyway — ' She indicated the large oak door in front of them. ' — I guess it's too late to chicken out now.'

Tiphanie nodded. 'Here we go, then.

Open Sesame.' She pushed open the door and stepped into the centre's reception area.

To her delight, Howard was there, talking to a younger man.

He looked over and then hurried towards her with his arms outstretched. 'Tiphanie! I hoped you'd be early. I've missed you so much.'

'Mmm, me too,' Tiphanie murmured, looking up at him as she slid her holdalls to the floor before returning his hug.

'I've checked your room number. I've collected your name badge, too.' He opened her jacket and pinned the badge onto her sweater.

She felt her cheeks turn pink, and he nodded and smiled. 'Just sign in at the desk, and we'll go and get you settled.'

'I can't just leave Felicity to find her own way round,' Tiphanie whispered.

'You won't have to. This is Liam . . .' Howard inclined his head towards the other man and then looked at Felicity.

'He's your number-one assistant by day and bartender by night,' he said. 'You'll show Felicity where everything is, won't you, Liam?'

'Be pleased to.' Liam looked appreciatively at Felicity.

'We'll sign in then, shall we, Felicity?' Tiphanie wriggled out of Howard's arms and stepped towards the desk.

As soon as they were out of earshot, she glanced at her friend. 'Sorry about Howard being so ... so ... ' She shrugged, then picked up a pen and wrote her details in the book.

'So eager.' Felicity rolled her eyes. 'Don't worry, I'll be fine. I've got the luscious Liam to look after me.'

'He's a bit young for you, isn't he?' teased Tiphanie.

'Young or not, it's about time I had a man in my life again.'

'Fliss? You wouldn't?'

'We-ell. You must admit, he's got a fantastic body.'

Tiphanie sneaked a look at Liam, who was standing with Howard. 'He's certainly got the cutest baby face,' she agreed. Then she caught Howard's eye, and nodded when she saw him pick up her bags and mouth, 'Hurry up.'

Howard didn't give her much time to get her bearings as he hustled her out of the reception hall and up the stairs.

'Hell, we should have collected your key,' he said when they reached her room.

Tiphanie turned the knob. 'It's OK, it's open,' she said.

Once inside, Howard dropped her bags and took her in his arms again. But when his hands wandered beneath her sweater, she pushed them away. 'Stop it,' she protested. 'Someone might come in.' Besides, Howard's eagerness worried her a little.

'Let's go to my rooms, then,' he said. 'Nobody will disturb us there. In fact, you might as well share with me.'

She swallowed a sigh. She wasn't too sure she wanted to deepen their relationship that far. 'I don't want to do that, Howard. I'd feel like everybody would know and start talking about us,' she added.

'So what? We're both free and over twenty-one. Don't be so virtuous. It won't matter if people talk.'

'It would matter to me. I'm here to work, and so are you,' she pointed out.

'We won't be working all through the night . . . oh, all right,' he added, clearly realising from her scowl that she'd meant what she'd said. 'You win. But only because, once the festival's over, we'll have the following week together, won't we, hmm?'

Now was the time to tell him something unexpected had happened and she'd be looking after her niece and nephew next week. 'Um, well — ' she began.

'Just the two of us alone in an isolated croft. There'll be all the time in the world for us to get to know each other properly, my little firebird.' He pulled her closer.

'No, Howard. I — '

He laughed. 'And I can't wait to — '

The sound of a meaningful cough halted Howard mid-sentence and had Tiphanie leaping out of his embrace. A tall, dark-haired figure was rising from the large couch which faced the window opposite the door.

A tall, dark, *piratical* figure, Tiphanie added silently to her first lightning impression as the man turned towards them and she took in the unruly hair, the dark chocolate-brown eyes, the high cheekbones and slightly mocking mouth, and caught a drift of cologne that reminded her of the scent of a sea breeze.

'I'm afraid this room has not yet been vacated.' There was a trace of laughter in his velvet-edged voice.

Howard opened his mouth, presumably about to apologise, but Tiphanie spoke before he could.

'What stopped you from telling us that sooner?' she demanded. 'Do you make a habit of listening in on private conversations? Were you hoping to hear something you could use in your next book? That's if you *are* a writer?' she added, as she realised he could be an artist for all she knew.

'I'll take the questions in order, shall I?' He seemed totally unfazed by Tiphanie's verbal attack. 'One, I was listening to music.' He made a light gesture at the headphones hanging round his neck. 'I was only aware of your intrusion, and the unasked for *irritainment*, when it ended.'

Tiphanie made an indignant sound and he raised an eyebrow before continuing with the hint of laughter back in his voice. 'Two, as soon as the CD ended and I heard voices, I let you know I was here.

'And three, as I'm a cartographer, from the snippet of conversation I did overhear, you needn't worry that it gave me inspiration.'

Tiphanie's bubbly sense of humour suddenly overtook her earlier embarrassment and anger. She knew a cartographer compiled or drew maps, but just couldn't resist replying with,

'No, I can see it wouldn't now I know you take cars' photos.'

She turned to grin at Howard. 'Whereas you,' she said, 'could use a scene like this in *Brawn and Bedlington*.'

But the amused, velvety voice hadn't stopped. Tiphanie wiped the smile from her face and shot its owner a withering glance.

'As I was saying, I believe ten o'clock was the time given for vacating the rooms, and it's only quarter to ten now. However . . . ' His eyes flicked to the badge declaring her name. ' . . . however, Ms Timpson, luckily I had the forethought to pack my belongings last night.'

His long jeans-clad legs made short work of the distance to the bed where a rucksack sat next to a large CD carrier. He picked them up, and the same fluid strides brought him towards the door. A smile ruffled his mouth as he glanced at Tiphanie, then he opened the door and went out.

'Exit Mr Sarky.' Tiphanie giggled. 'Sarky as in sarcastic,' she added, in case Howard hadn't understood.

Howard laughed. 'You weren't too bad on the sarcasm front yourself. It was obvious you were enjoying yourself, which is why I left the talking to you.'

'You left the talking to me because you were too busy taking mental notes, writing a new episode of *B & B* in your head,' she accused. 'And I reckon your fingers are itching to scribble them down.'

She decided not to tell him right now that the holiday was off. She'd wait until a better opportunity presented itself. After all, she reasoned, Howard owned the croft, so they'd be able to go some other time. They were both freelancers, they didn't have to book time off work.

'You know me too well,' he told her, dropping a swift kiss on her head. 'I could go and get it on paper while you're unpacking. I'll pick you up in fifteen minutes or so and give you the guided tour. Your first workshop's at two o'clock.'

★ ★ ★

The days flew past. Tiphanie found lecturing stimulating and rewarding — her students anxious to digest anything she could tell them. And the evenings spent with the other lecturers, discussing their various aspirations and eating the delicious meals provided by Felicity and her team, were inspiring and enjoyable.

Howard seemed to accept the fact that Tiphanie said goodnight, lingeringly yet firmly, at her own door, usually at an unearthly hour in the morning.

The right opportunity for her to break her news to Howard didn't seem to present itself; or maybe she guessed it would cast a blight on their enjoyment and didn't look too hard for an opportune time.

She finally broached the matter on

the morning of their last-but-one day, over breakfast.

'I can't come to the croft,' she told him apologetically. 'The twins' grandmother's got to go into hospital, and I'm the only one available to look after them.' Knowing she was gabbling, she continued, 'It won't be a chore, Zoe and Jack are nine now, and they're great kids. Anthony, their dad, would've been so proud of them,' she added sadly.

Tiphanie still missed her eldest brother so much — almost as much as she did her mum who'd been killed in the same plane crash five years ago. The twins' widowed mother, Fiona, had thrown herself into her work, trying to overcome her heartbreak, and travelled around the world with the orchestra she conducted. Fiona's mother willingly looked after the twins, helped whenever necessary by Anthony's side of the family. That often meant Tiphanie, but she didn't mind; she adored her niece and nephew.

Howard carried on eating. Tiphanie

crossed her fingers and continued hopefully, 'I'm taking them to Tristan's — he's got a place on the salt marshes. You could come, too. Tris will be there himself until Wednesday, and he'll take the twins on outings, so you and I would have plenty of time to ourselves. I haven't seen it yet, but I know it's in an isolated and beautiful area.'

Howard's knife and fork clattered on his plate. 'I'd have thought Tristan's responsibility towards the children would be greater than yours, Tiphanie. Their father was *his* twin, for heaven's sake. Why can't Tristan look after them until Wednesday, and then your other brother and his wife have them for the rest of the week?'

'Tristan's single, remember,' said Tiphanie. 'He enjoys taking the twins out, but he feels better with a woman around for bedtime and bathtime. And Tad and Linda have got houseguests all week.'

'Well, I'm fed up with your family problems intruding in our lives,' snapped Howard. 'You let your brothers use you as a doormat.'

'I do *not*. We're just there for each other, that's all.'

'Whatever.' Howard shrugged. 'But they're not wiping their feet on me. I'm going to the croft as planned. And I've a good mind to find someone else to go with me.'

That hurt. Didn't she mean anything to him after all?

'Go ahead and find someone, then,' she shot back over the splintering of her heart. 'I'm sure there'll be no shortage of volunteers to schmooze their way into the chance of writing or appearing in an episode of *Brawn and Bedlington*.' Then she jerked to her feet and, feeling as if there were lead weights inside her shoes, walked stiffly away to take her morning workshop.

Tiphanie didn't see Howard during the lunch hour, though she searched for him, wanting to apologise. They'd both said things they hadn't meant, hadn't they?

She caught sight of him going into his afternoon workshop, but he was surrounded by a crowd of eager students, and her own attendees were waiting for her.

The evening was spent in riotous partying amongst the lecturers; they'd all be leaving the next morning. Drink flowed freely, and everyone seemed to be having a good time. Tiphanie left them to it and went up to her room.

She felt hurt, angry, and rebellious all at once. Howard hadn't spoken one word to her, hadn't even looked her way. And to think she'd wanted to apologise for what she'd said this morning.

Perhaps it was a good thing she'd had to back out of the holiday? She'd been looking forward to it, though; the break from one of her families would have done her good.

Still, she'd had five days away from her real family. Her other family — her cartoon characters — was just what she needed right now. Working on them might help calm her down.

Her sketchpad and pencils were on the desk, her CD player beside them; she liked music to draw to, and it was a sort of tradition — or superstition — to play it on CDs rather than an iPod. Then she realised she'd left her CDs in the locker in her lecture room and she didn't feel like going back downstairs.

But she was notoriously untidy in any other matter save her work, and tended to shove things out of sight. It was more than likely she'd tucked a disc away somewhere. Eventually, she found one amongst her undies in the top drawer of the chest.

She put it into the CD player without looking at the title; she'd no story in mind, so it wouldn't matter what she listened to as long as it was something from her collection. All her music was carefully chosen for what she called its drawing rhythm.

Tiphanie instantly recognised the voice of one of her favourite singers, but she knew she hadn't got this

Maddy Prior number.

Reaching for the plastic cover, she scanned the information. Ironically, the song was titled 'Happy Families'. 'Think of the *Frolics*, not the Timpsons,' she muttered.

But it was no good — her real family kept intruding into her thoughts. Maybe Howard was right; maybe she did let them use her as a doormat. Maybe . . .

Tiphanie shrugged impatiently; it was the words of the song projecting her thoughts that way. For once she'd work in silence.

She was about to stop the CD when the phone rang. Every room had its own phone controlled by the switchboard in the main part of the hotel, and the soft double burr alerted her to the fact that it was an internal call.

Thinking it was Howard, who knew she always sketched her ideas to music, she changed her mind about stopping it. 'It'll do him good to think I feel carefree enough to be working,' she murmured, increasing the volume before she picked up the phone.

'Ms Timpson?'

She recognised the voice immediately. 'Speaking,' she replied brusquely.

'I can hear you've found my Maddy Prior?'

His deep-timbred tone sent a delicious shiver through her body. She was so surprised, she couldn't answer.

'I thought I must have left it there.' He paused again, as though waiting for some kind of response.

Tiphanie remained silent.

'Unfortunately,' he continued, 'circumstances forced me to vacate my room rather quicker than I'd planned, and . . . '

That hadn't sounded so deep and velvety. He was laughing at her, damn him.

' . . . I didn't have time for a final check to make sure I had everything. So — '

'You had time to eavesdrop on a private conversation though, didn't you,

Mr Sarky?' Tiphanie interrupted. 'And don't worry, I'll leave your disc at the reception desk before I leave.'

'No need for that. I had a meeting with my agent this evening, so I'm spending the night here in the hotel. I'll stroll over to the annexe in the morning and fetch it myself.'

'I'll leave it at the reception desk,' she repeated.

'You might be too busy thinking of your forthcoming holiday, just the two of you alone in that isolated croft.'

Tiphanie banged the phone down. 'There isn't going to be a holiday,' she yelled, glaring at it. 'In fact, there isn't going to be any anything.'

She wandered over to the couch and flopped onto it with a fretful sigh. Why couldn't Howard have understood? She'd told him Tris would be taking the twins out. They'd have had plenty of time to be alone together.

Putting her head back, she closed her eyes and relived Howard's harsh words. Surely he hadn't meant it when he said he'd find someone else to take to the croft? He was just lashing out because he was disappointed. If only she hadn't reacted the way she did, he'd probably have changed his mind.

I'll speak to him at breakfast tomorrow, she decided. I'll apologise, and try and persuade him to join me and the twins. He might feel apologetic himself in the morning. I'll wear the sweater and jeans I was wearing when we first met. He always says he loves me in them. I'll leave my hair loose and curly, the way he likes it, and spray on his favourite perfume.

Her decision made, she jumped up and went back to the desk. If she could manage to bury herself in work for an hour or so, it would tire her out and she'd sleep better.

The music was still loud and the words and the rhythm worked on her creative juices.

For the next three hours, stopping only to restart the CD when it ended, Tiphanie sketched out rough ideas for two episodes of *The Fenland Frolics*; their ups and downs of family life appeared every week in a national magazine.

At last, tiredness prevented her from sketching any more. After a quick shower she tumbled into bed; though, annoyingly, a rich, dark brown voice kept echoing in her mind.

'Why on earth am I thinking about Mr Sarky?' she muttered, thumping her pillow to try and drown the memory of his voice. 'He's despicable.'

But how strange that someone like him should enjoy Maddy Prior. She'd have thought something harsher and more vigorous would be more his taste.

She sent herself to sleep by silently reeling off titles of music that would suit the tall, lean, dark, piratical, sarcastic man.

* * *

Waking early, her only thoughts were of Howard. She lay for a while rehearsing what she'd say to him. Then suddenly she remembered he'd given her a spare key to his suite in case she'd change her mind about sharing it.

She'd never used the key; in fact, until a second ago she'd forgotten all about it. Now she'd remembered it, she thought it was a lucky omen.

Bounding out of bed, Tiphanie paused only to drag off her nightshirt, drag on the sweater and jeans Howard liked so much, and to spray herself with *Forever* before hurrying to his suite . . .

2

Champagne bucket in hand, Tiphanie crept into the bedroom and stared down at Howard. The sound of his deep, even breathing abounded; he was sleeping the sleep of the exhausted.

Slowly . . . carefully, her fingers trembling with the emotion spiralling through her body, Tiphanie eased down the sheet — the only thing covering him — then froze for a moment as he mumbled and turned over onto his back.

But he didn't wake.

The black silk slithered pleasingly, and she encouraged it to rest just below the top of his thighs. Her bare toes clenched the carpet. She could hear the echo of her heart pounding in her ears, and for a moment she allowed her eyes to linger . . . Then, shrugging, she tipped the bucket.

Her aim was deadly accurate.

The melting ice found its target.

'That's for cheating on me with my best friend,' she hissed over his anguished groans. And, swallowing down a hysterical giggle, she swirled round and marched out, closing the door firmly behind her.

The said best friend, still scantily clad — and, as of this morning, her ex-best friend — was now sitting bolt upright on a chair in the adjoining room. Actually wringing her hands, thought Tiphanie. Like a character in a farce. Next she'll be telling me it didn't mean anything.

'It didn't mean anything,' said Felicity.

'Just a *starter affair*, was it?' A short-lived affair that ended immediately with no regrets? She'd read that term in a magazine and was pleased she'd remembered it. Cool, Tiphanie, cool, she told herself.

'Howard was upset because you'd backed out of the holiday he'd arranged. We'd both had too much to drink and — '

'And he found comfort in your willing arms?'

'It's *you* he loves, Tizz, even though you always put your family before him.'

'That's why I came into his suite this morning.' Tiphanie's tone was bitter. 'I was going to try and explain things to him. I couldn't believe it when I saw you walking out of the bedroom carrying a tray and wearing almost nothing but a silly smile.'

She still couldn't quite believe it, but the evidence was there in front of her eyes. 'Even if you'd been fully dressed, that smile and the remains of your champagne breakfast would have given you away.'

Tiphanie paused to dump the empty ice bucket back on the depleted tray before she could give in to the temptation to ram it down over Felicity's head, but her anger was beginning to wane.

Dredging up the last of it, she continued, 'In case you're interested, I, thank heavens, never reached the stage of drinking champagne after a night of togetherness.'

'No. You never reach that stage with anyone,' said Felicity. 'Which is why you're known as the 'Frigid Flirt'.'

'Rather that than snatching every opportunity to get a man,' retorted Tiphanie as she stalked to the door.

However, once outside the suite, the hurt took over. Felicity and Howard. Howard and Felicity! How *could* they? She felt the tears pricking at the back of her eyelids and bit painfully on her lower lip.

He isn't worth crying over, she told herself firmly as, head down, she hurried towards the sanctuary of her own room.

Blindly, she felt for the door, and felt her hand pushing on something decidedly human instead.

'So he got his own way at last? All those maidenly protests were just an act and the firebird allowed herself to be captured.'

Tiphanie felt the colour flare in her cheeks at the sound of the low, rich brown voice. But she raised her head to meet the amused gaze of the speaker. 'That is so not true,' she said before she could stop herself.

Then, annoyed because she was aware her voice had trembled and she was aware of that drift of tantalising sea-breeze scent again, she said indignantly, 'What the hell are you doing here spying on me again? You told me last night you were staying in the main building . . . or are you just going back there after spending the night elsewhere?'

'If I had spent the night elsewhere, I'd have had the decency to get dressed before leaving,' he said, gesturing towards her bare feet.

'I wouldn't call bare feet indecent. Still, I suppose to a . . . a stuffed shirt like you, who'd doubtless wear shoes and socks to go paddling . . . '

Realising how unlikely it was that he would dream of doing anything as childish as paddling, with or without shoes and socks, Tiphanie broke off and tried to think of some other activity where shoes and socks would seem superfluous or ridiculous.

'Actually,' he said, as though she hadn't spoken, 'I came over to see if you were up yet. I did tell you I'd come and fetch my CD.'

'And I told you I'd leave it at the reception desk. I still intend to do that. You've had a wasted journey. Now, if you'd be so kind as to move, I want to get into my room.'

★   ★   ★

She tried to get behind him to open the door, but he moved swiftly, swivelling her around until she was facing him again. It was then he saw the single tear rolling down one flushed cheek. Before he could stop himself, he moved one hand from her shoulder and ran the pad of his thumb over the teardrop. She stared up at him, her smoky grey eyes wide like a curious kitten's, and he felt her warm breath on his throat. He dipped his head slightly . . .

★   ★   ★

For a brief moment, Tiphanie found herself holding her breath, waiting for his lips to touch hers. Then fury overrode all other feeling. She pushed him away with a strength she didn't know she possessed, and shot into her room locking the door behind her.

Breathing deeply, she forced her trembling legs to move to the bed. She sank down onto the edge of it and buried her face in her hands. In less than ten minutes she'd lost her current man and her lifelong best friend, and been almost ravished by a virtual stranger.

No. She wouldn't think of *him*. She'd think of what she'd done to Howard.

Momentarily, a smile found its way through her hurt as she tried to imagine how Howard would have felt when the melting ice cubes so rudely disturbed his satiated sleep.

Then she shook her head in despair, and the smile disappeared when she thought of Felicity, and her former friend saying something about she wanted a man in her life again. She needn't have put herself forward as man-bait for Howard, though. Even if she'd had too much to drink, it was still unforgivable.

Maybe Howard had been the one to make the first move. He certainly wasn't blameless. Well, good riddance to him. She'd miss him, but not half as much as she'd miss Fliss.

'Hell, I'm overemotional, overwrought, and over everything,' Tiphanie sighed, angrily brushing away the tears which had started to creep down her cheeks.

A frisson ran through her body as she further realised that she was remembering the touch of a gentle thumb. Jumping up, she went to the hand basin and splashed cold water over her burning face, trying to erase the memory of that and everything else that had happened as well.

Thank heavens there are no work-shops this morning, she thought as she spooned coffee into the cafetière and waited for the kettle to boil. She needn't stay for the winding-up speeches. She'd drink her coffee, pull herself together, and then leave. She'd spend the weekend quietly with her father, and on Monday she'd be taking the twins to Tristan's and they'd enjoy exploring somewhere they had never been before.

She concentrated determinedly on thinking up things she and Tristan could do with their niece and nephew the following week, refusing to allow entry to any other thoughts as she sipped the strong, bitter drink. She felt less keyed up when she'd drained her second cup.

Swiftly, she changed into different clothes. The outfit Howard liked so much could go to a charity shop. Then she started to pack her belongings into her holdalls. She took far more trouble in folding the clothes than was necessary, but her slow, methodical actions further calmed her.

Hoping and praying she wouldn't meet anyone on the way, she strode down to the lecture room to retrieve the discs she'd left in the locker, then hurried back to place them alongside her CD player in the carrying box designed to protect them.

Her hand wavered over the Maddy Prior disc; she really should leave it at the reception desk. But the thought she might bang into Mr Sarky decided her against that. She wouldn't go into the main building at all; she'd leave the key in her room and post the disc back to the hotel, asking them to forward it to the previous occupant of Room Fifteen.

She had no idea what his real name was; he'd always be 'Mr Sarky' in her mind. 'Not that I'll ever think of him again once I've left this place,' she murmured.

A worried frown creased Tiphanie's

brow as she walked briskly out of the Conference Centre and across to where she'd parked her car. She'd had Felicity for company on the way down — who would have thought they would not be going back together as well?

Tiphanie wasn't worried about how Felicity would get home. What bothered her was the fact that *she* would be in the car by herself.

I'll be perfectly all right on my own, she told herself firmly, as she put her luggage in the boot. It's morning, not night, and the car was serviced last week. As long as I check I've got enough petrol, I won't have to stop until I get to King's Lynn. There's a car phone in this car, and my mobile is fully charged as well.

But once she was sitting in the car, with the empty passenger seat mocking her, the memories of three years ago played on her mind . . .

She'd been driving along a lonely Fenland road on a dark and misty evening. The car she'd been driving then — an old banger she refused to let go of because it had been her mum's, but one which should really have been in the scrap metal place in the sky — had broken down. And she'd been unable to phone for help because she'd forgotten to charge her mobile.

When a figure materialised out of the mist, knocked on her car window, and indicated she should open the door, she'd been scared witless — she'd read about awful things happening to lone women drivers on country lanes such as this. She'd watched him try the car door handle, but luckily, she'd already locked herself in. He'd walked around the car, trying all the doors, before coming back to the driver's side. After banging his palm hard against her window, he'd said something; but, apart from a couple of swear words, she couldn't tell what. Then he'd disappeared into the mist.

She could never remember how long she'd sat there, trembling and thinking about what could have happened if she'd not managed to lock the car doors, but she could remember screaming when a policeman had tapped on the window to see if she needed help. She hadn't even seen or heard the police car pull up behind her.

She'd spent a couple of days in hospital suffering from shock. Her family had rallied round with love and sympathy, though her twin brother's brisk: 'You were lucky this time, Tiphanie, and maybe you'll stop hanging on to things out of sentiment and remember to keep your mobile charged as well,' had been the 'cruel to be kind' advice that helped her to pull herself together . . .

Tad had also bought her this car and had the phone installed, but even now she had to psych herself up to drive alone on a long journey. And even though nothing awful had happened on that misty evening, thoughts of what could have done still preyed on her mind. She had to psych herself up, too, when it came to intimacy. No matter how much she wanted to love and be loved, it was hard not to freeze. She'd been starting to overcome this fear with Howard . . .

But all of it is history now. Just start the car, Tiphanie.

'It isn't such a long journey,' she assured herself, staring at her reflection in the driving mirror.

The early morning sun danced over the bright red hair which made her so noticeable. She reached into the glove compartment for the dull head-scarf she always kept there, and after tying it on turban-style she felt less conspicuous.

★　★　★

Two hours later, Tiphanie drew up outside a large Victorian house. This was where she and her brothers had grown up, and where she'd returned to live after the plane crash. Dad had needed her at that time, and she'd been so close to her mother they both thought they'd be able to help each other through the grieving of their double loss.

As she walked up the path she noticed that the grey pussy-willow buds had burst into bright yellow heads of fluffy pollen in her absence. Deep mauve ground ivy was creeping up the low garden wall, and primroses fought for breathing space amongst the tangled roots.

Spring has arrived, she thought, and the thought caused pain: spring was for lovers.

Sighing deeply, she opened the front door, then bent down to pick up a bottle of milk from the doorstep. They were lucky still having a milk delivery in this area — but maybe it was a new milkman because . . . 'Only one pint,' she muttered. 'We usually have four on a Saturday.'

Once inside, the first thing she noticed was the small pile of luggage in the hall. The second thing was the ladders, planks, and tins of paint. And the hall furniture was covered with dustsheets.

A plaintive meow caused her to look upwards. Marmaduke, her marmalade cat, was crouching miserably on top of the covered grandfather clock, swishing his tail angrily. Tiphanie put the bottle of milk and her holdalls down, pulled the hall chair with their family crest on from under its sheet, and positioned it carefully.

She knew from experience that her five-foot-one length couldn't stretch itself to reach the top of the clock. She also knew from experience that Marmaduke would hurl himself off the clock when it struck the hour.

But Tiphanie didn't want to wait; she wanted the comfort of her cat in her arms now.

'There, there, Duke,' she soothed, as she successfully lifted the big cat. 'What's going on, then? Whose is the luggage, and what is all this decorating stuff doing here? Never mind, I'll find out soon enough.'

She stepped down from the chair and buried her face in the cat's long fur. 'Oh, Duke, I'm so miserable,' she whispered. 'Miserable and angry,' she added, wandering into the kitchen.

'Well, you never did like Howard, did you? You'll be glad that we won't be seeing him again. And, soon, so will I,' she said firmly, putting the cat down and taking off her headscarf.

'All right, I can see your saucer's empty, I'll pour you some milk.' She opened the fridge only to discover that there wasn't any milk there. Feeling puzzled, she walked back to the hall. 'I can't understand why the milkman only left one pint,' she said as she picked the bottle up.

'Because we'll only need enough for Marmaduke and a couple of cups of coffee,' came her father's voice from the stairs.

'I'm glad you got back earlier than I expected, Tiphanie,' he added as he hurried down to embrace her. 'I'm going to Carrickfergus for a few days.

Professor Alleyn phoned and asked if I'd like to collaborate with him on a tract he's writing on King John. It was too good a chance to miss; I'm actually working on King John myself. You know, it's the series I'm writing for the Schools Programmes?'

'Tell me about it in the kitchen,' said Tiphanie. 'Marmaduke is waiting for his milk.'

'I'm leaving in about an hour,' her father continued, as Tiphanie bent to fill Marmaduke's saucer. 'Tristan's coming to pick you up this afternoon to take you to his place. I don't suppose you saw him on television last night? Promoting his latest Tristan Simpton book. I still can't understand why his real name wasn't good enough for him. He even changed it by deed poll and uses 'Simpton' all the time.'

Her father paused and Tiphanie addressed his last comments first. 'You know Tris didn't want any comparisons made to your writing, Dad. Neither did he want any favours granted because he's got a famous father. I always thought it was rather clever using an anagrammatical version of our surname.

'But what do you mean, he's picking me up this afternoon? He's supposed to be phoning me tomorrow with the directions to his place. You do remember that I'm taking the twins there on Monday?'

'You can't stay here,' he replied. 'Not even for the weekend. The decorators arrived earlier than expected. All the wallpaper's stripped off upstairs, and in the lounge and the sitting room, so we had to change the plans. Tristan will fill you in on the new ones when he gets here.'

'Which were made without consulting me,' said Tiphanie. 'Honestly, Dad, the pair of you are impossible. I've done enough driving for today. I really don't want to go to Tris's before Monday. I'll go upstairs and see how bad things are.'

'You'll get a shock,' he warned. 'There must have been at least six layers of paper on every wall. The lounge and dining room are the same. The staircase, my study, the hall and the kitchen are the only untouched places. And don't get any bright ideas about sleeping in my study.'

Her father hadn't exaggerated, she acknowledged gloomily as she made her inspection. There was no way she could stay here.

'OK, you're right,' she said bitterly when she returned to the kitchen. 'I'll have to go to Tristan's.'

'I've left his address and phone number with Madge in case of emergencies — pointless giving her Professor Alleyn's, we'll be touring. Madge will be coming in every day to tidy up after the decorators and keep an eye on things.'

Tiphanie wasn't interested in that information; she was working things out.

'I'll have to follow Tristan in my car and come back for the twins on Monday. After all,' she added, picking

Marmaduke up from the table where he was sitting cleaning himself after his milk, 'it's par for the course — everything else has gone wrong today.'

'I thought you looked peaky,' said her father. 'What's happened to upset you, pet?'

She sat down, cradling Marmaduke in her arms. 'Howard and I are no longer — and don't sympathise, Dad, I don't want to start howling. I think I'll go and . . . and — '

'You'll do nothing except sit there while I make you some hot chocolate,' he commanded. 'It's more comforting than coffee. It will make you feel better.'

That almost made Tiphanie smile. Though her dad was often absent-minded, living in the past with his historical characters, when something happened to upset her he came back into the present. Well, maybe not quite the present, she thought, as she watched him spoon chocolate powder into a mug. He'd spoken as though she was still five instead of twenty-five-going-on-twenty-six.

'I don't like to see you hurting, pet,' he said, putting the drink on the table.

'No sympathy, remember,' she warned lightly, burying her face in Marmaduke's fur. 'I'll soon recover. My heart isn't broken, just bruised.'

What bruised it as much as anything is the impression Mr Sarky got of me, she realised in silent amazement. He thought I'd spent the night with Howard. And then, there I was wanting *him* to kiss me. I wonder if he knew that.

Stop thinking about him, she cautioned herself. You'll never see him again. And you don't want to, either, she added.

'I'm going to steer clear of all men,' she said aloud, looking at her father.

'Yes, pet,' he agreed, 'if you say so. But now I'd better finish getting ready,' he added. 'My taxi will be here soon, I must make sure I've got all my notes, and . . . '

He's back to being absent-minded, thought Tiphanie, as her father mumbled his way out of the kitchen, leaving her to finish her drink alone.

⋆   ⋆   ⋆

'You look terrible, Tiphanie,' Tristan greeted her with brotherly candour when he stepped into the hall.

'Thanks,' she grimaced. 'I don't think I look too bad considering . . . '

'Considering what?' He eyed her thoughtfully. 'Fallen out with Howard, have you?'

'You could say that,' she replied offhandedly, turning to step over the tins of paint and the planks.

'Good job you're coming to my place, then,' said Tristan, following her into the kitchen. 'A change of scenery and all that will work wonders.'

'It's the change of timing that's bothering me. I wanted to stay here over the weekend and bring the twins down on Monday. Not come to yours today and then have to come back for them.'

'All that's taken care of. Oh, good, I see you've got coffee perking as usual.' Tristan poured himself a cup, sat on the edge of the table, and continued, 'Didn't Dad tell you?' He shook his head. 'Silly question, really. Tad's driving Jack and Zoe down to my place early tomorrow morning, to save you having to make a double journey on Monday.'

At the mention of her twin, Tiphanie muttered, 'I might have guessed Tad had something to do with these new plans.'

Tristan grinned. 'He's driving them down in your car. He'll be here soon to fetch it. Then he's going to the airport to pick up the German family he and Linda are hosting. That's why they couldn't have Zoe and Jack, remember? Because of their visitors.'

'I suppose Tad has lent Linda his car, and he wants to use mine tonight?' Tiphanie said icily. 'Bringing the twins down tomorrow is just soft-soaping me. Never mind what I might have planned, you lot just went ahead and organised me to suit yourselves.

'Howard was right. You do treat me like a doormat. And I'm willing to bet there was some ulterior motive when you suggested I brought the twins to your place instead of looking after them in their own home. And don't turn your back and pretend to be pouring more coffee. You can't possibly have finished your first cup yet.'

'You know,' said her brother, turning round to face her with a grin on his face, 'your hair always seems to go even more orange when you yell. It's the same colour as Marmaduke's fur. Shall I put him into his travelling box while there's a chance?'

He reached over, picked the cat up from the window ledge where he'd been sleeping in the sun, and said to him, 'You'll be pleased to see your mum again, won't you?'

'How is Chrysanthemum?' asked

Tiphanie, diverted for the moment. 'I hope she'll pose for me like Marmaduke does. I can feature her in the *Fenland Frolics* then.'

'She's fine now, thanks to a marvellous cat therapist.'

'Cat therapist? What on earth are you talking about, Tris?'

'I'll tell you later. Are you all packed? Tad will be here soon, and I want to get straight off when he comes. I'd like us to arrive in daylight. Find me Marmaduke's box, I'll see to him while you fetch your things.'

'All this busying around isn't fooling me, Tristan. There's something you're not telling me.'

But her brother just smiled.

Tiphanie shrugged and then made her way upstairs to finish repacking her holdalls with clean clothes.

When she got back downstairs, Tad had already been and gone. Which was perhaps a good thing, thought Tiphanie, because she'd probably have given him a piece of her mind too.

⋆ ⋆ ⋆

'Wake up, Tiphanie. We're almost there.'

'We are? How long was I asleep?'

'Only for twenty minutes or so. It's easy to miss the turn-off: I thought I'd better wake you so you could familiarise yourself with the landmarks,' Tristan explained.

Tiphanie yawned and stretched. 'No rush for that. You'll be here until Wednesday.'

But, curious about the area, she looked through the car window. 'Is that a farm over there, Tris?'

'Yes. Almost my nearest neighbour. That track off to the right leads to the farm, and this one we're on leads eventually to my place. We're just crossing over the River Nund,' he added.

Once over the bridge, he drove a few yards further and then brought the car to a halt in front of a five-barred gate.

'Miles and miles of grey, blue and

51

green,' Tiphanie murmured appreciatively. 'It's lonely but beautiful.'

'See that cottage across the river?' Tristan pointed. 'My nearest neighbour lives there . . . '

Tiphanie glanced cursorily at the small single-storey cottage huddled behind a straggly hedge and surrounded by a clump of bent trees. Then she focused her attention on their side of the river.

'If that's your nearest neighbour, then *where* is your place? I can't see anything this side . . . only that funny stump-shaped building guarded by a big tree. It looks like a candle in a saucer. But what's it for?'

'You'll see soon enough.' Her brother laughed. 'Hop out and open the gate, Tizz. But be careful, it's always breezy down here, and the gate has a habit of blowing itself out of your hands.'

Tiphanie got out and stood against the car for a moment. She could smell salt in the air and feel it on her face and in her hair, which was flying out like crazy orange streamers as the wind blew it every which way.

Laughing at the sudden carefreeness overtaking her, she hurried forward to battle with the gate.

'We'll walk from here,' called Tristan, getting out of the car with Marmaduke's travelling box as she slipped the rusty chain over the gatepost. 'And Tizz, look who's coming to meet us.'

'It's Chrysanthemum,' observed Tiphanie, joining Tristan and poking a finger through one of the air holes in Marmaduke's box. 'Duke, Mum's here.'

'I don't call her Mum, or even just Chrys any more,' said Tristan as Tiphanie got her holdalls out of the car. 'She answers to Crystal now,' he continued as they began walking along the river bank towards his cat. 'You see, when I first moved, she just wouldn't settle. I ended up consulting a cat therapist, I mentioned her earlier. Anyway, she suggested changing Chrysanthemum's name to Crystal, and using her full name all the time. So that's what I did and she's been fine ever since.'

'You're ridiculous.' Tiphanie laughed as she watched the cat stroll towards them, her long fur ruffling in the wind, her tail swaying from side to side. 'But how far has she come? I still can't see your house. Aren't you worried Mum — '

Tiphanie felt her brother's warning look and shrugged. 'All right. I'll call her Crystal. Aren't you worried she'll get lost?'

'Actually . . . ' Tristan chuckled. ' . . . I live here.' He waved his free hand. 'In the 'candle in a saucer', I think you called it.'

Tiphanie had just bent to pick Crystal up; rising with the cat in her arms, she turned to stare in amazement. 'Close up, it looks like a windmill without its sails,' she spluttered.

'You're almost spot on. It started life way back in the eighteen-hundreds as a smock or drainage mill to control the

54

level of the water on the marshes. It became redundant in the nineteen-fifties, and was renovated and converted into this about twenty years ago. The new owners, not very originally, named it Marsh View. I think there were plans to build a more conventional house or bungalow adjoining it.'

'I'm glad that didn't happen; it's great as it is.'

Tristan nodded. 'Cool, isn't it? My studio's right at the top. Crystal loves sitting on the window-sills and looking out over the mud-flats, though it was a couple of weeks before I could get her to go up the staircase. There's a basement, too, but no way will Crystal go through the basement door and down the steps.

'To be honest, Crystal is the reason I suggested you bring the twins here. I didn't want to put her into a cattery while I'm away. She mustn't be unsettled again.'

Marmaduke suddenly let out a long, angry yowl and started scratching at his box. 'Come on,' said Tris, hurrying down what served as a garden path. 'Let's go in and let Duke out.'

They walked up four stone steps to a wooden door. Tristan opened it, then stood back and ushered his sister in. 'No hall, as you can see. This is the lounge-cum-dining room.'

'It's fantastic,' said Tiphanie. And, as she carefully lifted her pet from his box, Crystal wound herself round and around her legs making gentle meowing noises.

'OK, you want to say hello to your son, don't you, Mum ... I mean, Crystal? There you go.' She lowered Marmaduke to the floor and the cats greeted each other ecstatically.

'So you like it, do you?' Tristan asked.

'I suppose you have got all mod cons?' Tiphanie asked suspiciously.

'There's running water, electricity ... you can't always get a signal for a mobile but, as you know, there's a landline. There's the phone in here and one in the studio. The kitchen's reasonably modern, though the cooker's run off Calor gas. The door Marmaduke's making his way to is the kitchen.' Tristan pointed to an arched door leading off the lounge and then waved a hand towards a narrow, winding stairway at the far side of the front door. 'Three bedrooms on the next storey, bathroom on the one after; and right at the top, as I told you outside, is my studio.'

'It's the bathroom I'm most interested in right now,' admitted Tiphanie. 'Come on, Mum — I mean, Crystal — show me the way. Are you coming up, Duke?'

'He's more interested in the food dishes,' Tristan said from the kitchen doorway. 'I'll feed him and Crystal and make us a drink while you're up there.'

However, Tiphanie returned sooner than he expected. 'Tristan,' she wailed, and he dashed back into the lounge to see his sister with a flushed and anguished face.

'Spider in the bath?' he asked.

'Noo-oo. My zip's stuck and my skin's caught in it.' She turned her back to her brother. She always wore jeans which zipped up at the back — she found front fastenings uncomfortable when leaning over her drawing board. 'Unjam it, Tris. It's agony.'

'You'll have to lie down,' Tristan said with a sigh, after jiggling fruitlessly at the zip for a few seconds.

She moaned loudly as she gingerly lowered herself to the floor and then Tristan knelt over her.

'Ow, ow, owww!' she groaned. 'I can't stand this.'

'You shouldn't wear such tight jeans, Tizz.' Tristan panted as he struggled with the zip.

'Never mind that. Just hurry, Tris. Please hurry,' Tiphanie gasped throatily and raised her head slightly, closing her eyes against the pain.

'Oh, I'm sorry. I've obviously called at the wrong time. But fancy meeting you here, Ms Timpson.'

When she heard that deep brown voice, Tiphanie wondered if she was dreaming. Her zip was free now. She opened her eyes and, clutching at her jeans, scrambled to her feet, staring in disbelief at the tall, dark, piratical man leaning nonchalantly against the front door.

3

'I take it you two have already met?'
said Tristan as he rose to his feet. 'I was
just unjamming her zip,' he explained to
the unexpected visitor.

He glanced at Tiphanie. 'Kyle lives in
that cottage on the other side of the
river, Tizz. It's nice that you two already
know each other.' He looked back at
Kyle. 'Tiphanie's my — '

Tiphanie didn't give her brother time
to finish what he'd been about to say.
'Oh, Mr Sarky and I have never been
formally introduced,' she said, aware of
the colour flaring in her cheeks as she
looked up, a long way up, to meet the
scornful deep brown eyes.

Then those very eyes raked her from
head to foot, before moving insolently
back up her body — pausing meaningfully at her hands which were gripping
her jeans tightly. And, because of that

perusal, Tiphanie guessed he had no idea Tristan was her brother.

As if confirming the fact, Kyle passed the book he was holding to Tristan. 'I only came to return your book.'

It was, Tiphanie noticed, one Tristan had written; his name, 'Tristan Simpton', emblazoned across the cover.

'I did knock,' Kyle continued, 'but understandably you didn't hear me. I wasn't aware you were . . . '

He paused and glanced again at Tiphanie before resuming. 'I wasn't aware you were entertaining. I'll leave you to it.'

'I . . . we . . . ' Tristan started to correct the conclusion Kyle had obviously drawn from the situation but he was too late. Kyle had wrenched the front door open and was striding out.

'His name isn't Sarky, it's Cooper,' stated Tristan in puzzlement, as the tall lean figure passed rapidly in front of the lounge window. 'He seemed to think — '

'That's his trouble. He sees or hears

things, and *thinks* he's drawn the right conclusions,' Tiphanie said flatly. 'And every time, he uses the lowest form of wit. Sarcasm. Hence, Mr Sarky. This is the fourth time it's happened.'

'I did try to tell him I was unjamming your zip,' said Tristan. 'And I was about to say you were my sister when you interrupted. Knowing you, that was because you were still mad at him because of whatever happened at your previous meetings?'

Tiphanie just glowered silently.

'So,' continued her brother, 'you can't really blame him if he thinks we were . . . were . . . ' He broke off, clearly choking back a laugh.

'I'm glad you think it's funny, because I don't,' Tiphanie spoke through clenched teeth.

'You know?' said Tristan. 'I wouldn't mind betting Kyle was envying me. Even though you are my sister, I have to admit you look beautiful when you're angry. I think he — '

'I'm not the slightest bit interested in

hearing what you think he thought or felt,' she said. 'It would be a waste of time and energy.'

'I'll believe you, thousands wouldn't,' said Tristan, laughing again as she walked out of the room.

Tiphanie's whole body felt as though it were on fire as she hurried up the winding stairs. In spite of her words to Tris, that annoying man — or rather, what he so obviously thought of her — was preying on her mind.

'Though I don't see why it matters what he thinks of me,' she told herself crossly as she reached her destination. And there was no way she'd be seeing him again — he wasn't likely to come visiting Tris while she was here.

It wasn't disappointment she felt at that last thought, was it? Why should she care if she never saw his mocking face again? A hawk-like face, hard-boned and masculine, a sensual mouth — at least, it would be when it wasn't set in disapproving lines. A mouth with a tiny scar at the right-hand corner.

He had the kind of hands she liked, she'd noticed when he'd handed the book to Tristan; noticed the covering of dark hair that sprinkled them and continued onto his arms. She hadn't been aware of what his hands or arms looked like previously, but this time his sleeves had been rolled back and, on one wrist, a heavy gold chain had glinted.

She shook her head impatiently. She didn't like jewellery on men. But his gold chain had only added to his masculinity as it nestled tantalisingly amongst the dark hair.

'There's nothing tantalising about Kyle,' she whispered despairingly. 'Nothing at all. You're seeing him through an artist's eyes, that's all.'

And how come she was thinking of him as 'Kyle' instead of 'Mr Sarky', which suited him much better?

* * *

'I think I'll go over to Kyle's cottage and put him straight,' said Tristan, when Tiphanie walked back into the lounge.

'Why bother?' she flared. 'I don't care if he thinks I'm a loose woman. I don't care what he thinks of me.'

'Well, well, he has got under your skin,' observed Tristan.

'Oh, stop going on about him, I don't want to talk about him. He's despicable. Tell me something about the local sights, Tris. Places we can take Zoe and Jack.'

'All right, but there are a couple of things you should know. Kyle doesn't like to be interrupted by anything at all when he's writing, and — '

'Writing?' interrupted Tiphanie. 'He told me he was a cartographer.'

'He did some cartography workshops a couple of weeks ago,' said Tristan. 'Is that when you met him?'

Tiphanie nodded. 'Sort of.'

'He's a man of many talents,' Tristan continued. 'He's a psychologist, but he gave that up and, recently, he's turned his hand to writing verses for greetings cards and short stories — though, like cartography, he sees that as a hobby.

'But, Tizz, this is important.' He waved a hand towards Marmaduke and Crystal, who'd clearly enjoyed their food and had now settled in the lounge to wash their whiskers. 'He can't stand cats. Whatever you do, don't let either of these two go over the bridge to his cottage.'

'I might have known he wouldn't like cats. A man like that just — '

'I thought you didn't want to talk about him?' Tristan interrupted teasingly.

I don't, she wailed silently, going over to pick Marmaduke up. And I don't want to think about him either.

But she kept thinking about him all evening, and during the night, he filled her dreams.

He was the first person she saw in the morning when she looked out of her bedroom window. He was jogging along his side of the river bank, and something clenched inside her stomach as she watched the graceful movements of his long, lean body.

Then she saw her car. Tad and the twins were here. Something to take my mind off Mr Sarky, she thought as she hurried down the twisty stairs and outside to greet them.

As so often happened when she hadn't seen Tad for a while, Tiphanie felt an acute sense of loss as she watched him get out of the car. He reminded her so much of Anthony. Especially now, when Tad was more or less the same age as Anthony had been when he'd lost his life in the plane crash.

It was a strange thing, because Tad was *her* twin — Anthony had been Tristan's. But Tad's looks and mannerisms were just like Anthony's used to be. Even Zoe and Jack, when they were little, had sometimes got mixed up about which one was their father and which one was Tad. And for a while after Anthony's death, when Tad visited his niece and nephew, Zoe had often called him 'Dad' before remembering he couldn't be because her dad was in heaven.

Shaking off her sad feelings, Tiphanie hurried forward to hug the three of them. 'Tris said you were coming early,' she said. 'But I didn't expect it to be before breakfast.'

'And we didn't expect to be living in a windmill for a week,' Zoe said, staring at it with big, round eyes.

'It's not a working windmill, Zo,' said Jack. 'It's not got sails. It's cool, though, isn't it?'

Tad grinned at the twins before looking at Tiphanie. 'We're early because I thought, as Tris is going up north tomorrow, Zoe and Jack would enjoy having one full day with both of you first,' he said.

'Sorry, Tizz,' said Tristan, who'd just joined them. 'I never got round to telling you I'm leaving a few days earlier, did I?'

So that was what he hadn't told her. Tiphanie shrugged. It wasn't worth commenting on. It wouldn't make that much difference, Tris leaving the next day instead of Wednesday.

She smiled mock-sweetly at him. 'In that case, Tristan, you can do all the cooking today. Starting with breakfast.'

'And then, while you're getting lunch, Tizz and the twins can drive me to the station,' said Tad.

Guessing that was her twin's way of supporting her — and, at the same time, ordering her about — Tiphanie ignored him and turned to her niece and nephew. 'Come on,' she said, 'I'll show you around.'

'Around the round rooms,' Zoe said, giggling.

The day passed quickly and busily. Tiphanie had no time to think about Tristan's annoying neighbour across the river.

And, to her relief, when she woke the next morning, she realised she hadn't dreamed about him, either.

★　★　★

'But Tris, you've got to help me get him down.' There were stone ledges circling the building about half a metre below all the windows. Tiphanie was staring up at the one below the studio windows where Marmaduke was sitting. 'He must have climbed the tree and then jumped over to the ledge,' she said.

'Sorry, Tizz, I can't help. I'll miss my train if I don't go now. Besides, he knows how to get down. He'll jump back over to the tree when he's ready. He did the same thing yesterday while you and the twins drove Tad to the station. The ledge is quite wide so he can't fall off.'

'But . . . but . . . '

'If you're bothered about him climbing back down the tree, open the studio windows,' said Tristan. 'He'll get in that way, then. Stop worrying about him. He'll be fine.'

'You're a good one to talk about not worrying,' she fumed, pummelling Tristan's chest. 'You actually consulted a cat therapist about Chrysanthemum-who's-now-got-to-be-called-Crystal. You've even left me the therapist's phone number in case *your* cat behaves strangely while you're away.'

'Well, if Marmaduke doesn't come down the tree, or refuses to climb in through a window, you can phone the therapist and ask her advice.' Tristan laughed as he fended off his sister's blows. 'I'll phone you in a few days and let you know when I'm returning, Tizz. You might . . . er . . . you might have to stay longer than a week. But I'll bring you a present back,' he whispered annoyingly in her ear.

Then, releasing her arms, he hurriedly dived into his car and started it up. 'Don't bother about the gate, I'll see to it,' he called through the car window.

By the time his words 'You might have to stay longer than a week' had sunk in, he was halfway to the gate.

Tiphanie started to run after the car, and then stopped as she heard a mocking 'Good morning' from the other side of the river.

Oh, great! I bet he saw me thumping Tris. What conclusion will he draw from that?

She tried to glare. Would he be able to see that from where he was? she wondered, taking in his v-necked tee-shirt and brief shorts. She eyed him up and down, taking in every part of him, and finally her gaze lingered on the harsh planes of his face emphasised by the early morning sun. Her insides jangled and she felt her pulse leap.

Surely she wasn't attracted to him, was she?

Tiphanie met his deep brown gaze, even as the river flowed between them. For a moment, that gaze captured her and held her prisoner. Then he was moving again, jogging rhythmically towards his cottage.

Angry with him for creating these feelings within her, angry with herself for allowing them, she spun round and flounced back to see if Marmaduke had moved yet.

He hadn't. Leaning against the tree, resplendent in its new spring greenery, she stared up at her pesky cat sitting on the ledge and wondered at the primeval recognition Kyle aroused in her.

'Maybe he's caught me on the rebound,' she muttered.

Rebound from what? demanded her inner voice. Howard never made you feel like this.

Could Kyle have been the reason I wouldn't give into Howard's pleas?

Did I stop feeling anything at all for Howard after that first morning at Lanleigh? I certainly noticed Kyle's eyes then . . . and his mouth and his long legs.

'To say nothing of his sarcasm,' she reminded herself, trying to re-conjure a feeling of dislike. And how come she was thinking of him as 'Kyle' again instead of 'Mr Sarky'?

Hell, how come she was thinking of him at all?

Way up on the ledge, Marmaduke moved. Tiphanie held her breath, her thoughts now all for her pet. 'Oh, Duke, don't try and jump down from there.'

The cat peered down, as if measuring the distance to the ground; and then, with a loud meow, he stiffened his legs, arched his back and froze like a cartoon cat.

'Tiphanie. Why didn't you wake us? We wanted to see Tristan off.' The twins, both with hair as orange as Tiphanie's — though their father, Anthony, had been as blond as Tristan, *his* twin, and their mother's hair was as black as a raven's — came running towards her. Then, obviously seeing her worried gaze, they followed that gaze to the ledge.

'Which cat is it?' gasped Zoe. 'I can't tell from here if it's Mum . . . I mean, Crystal . . . or Marmaduke.'

'It's Duke.' Tiphanie's voice wavered as they stared up. 'He's got a knack for finding his way to ungettable-at places. The trouble is, he hasn't got the same knack for getting himself down again.

He just freezes with fright.'

'The studio windows open, don't they?' Jack said. 'He's in between two of them. Let's go inside and see if we can coax him in.'

There were four windows in the circular studio. Tristan's cat was sitting by one, staring out across the mud-flats. 'We'd better not open that one or she might climb out of it,' Zoe said. 'But we could open the other three. We'll each of us stand by one and call Marmaduke. Mum might help by meowing.'

'Zoe,' snapped Tiphanie, 'for heaven's sake, remember to call her Crystal. Tristan says her old names unsettle her, and I don't want two unsettled cats to deal with.

'I think we'll just open one window for starters,' she continued. 'And I'll put some music on, one of the playlists on my CDs I made to work to. Marmaduke might come in then: he'll think I want him to pose for me.'

Tiphanie studied her discs. 'This one

will do. It starts with the Prelude to Act Three of *Lohengrin*. Marmaduke likes Wagner.'

'It's a shame you haven't got that Scarlatti harpsichord sonata . . . the 'Cat's Fugue' . . . it's supposed to represent a cat picking its way along a keyboard.' Jack chuckled. 'Duke might think it represents the windmill's ledge and pick his way along it till he reaches the open window.'

'What about 'I Taut I Taw a Puddy Tat'?' suggested Zoe.

'Don't start a game of Connections now,' ordered Tiphanie, turning the volume up. The twins had a marvellous knowledge of music and literature, and frequently aired it in their favourite game — finding something which connected to an action, or led on from something someone said.

'I mean it, I'm serious.' Tiphanie glared at them before peering out of the window she'd opened.

'Duke's moving,' she hissed after a few moments. 'Turn the volume right up, Jack. Oh no, he's turning himself around . . . Oh, sh — -*shampoo*, I can't bear to . . . Whew. He's OK . . . he's going towards the window nearest you, Zoe. Open it slowly so you don't frighten him.'

'You nearly said a swear word then, Tiphanie.' Jack wagged a finger.

'He's gone and sat down again,' reported Zoe, as the Prelude from *Lohengrin* came to an end. 'He's washing himself, Tiphanie. I don't think he's at all frightened.'

Tiphanie's playlist was an eclectic mix; suddenly Barbara Streisand was belting out 'Who's Afraid of the Big Bad Wolf?'.

'Marmaduke certainly isn't.' Jack laughed and, opening his window, made gentle howling noises to see if Marmaduke would move. 'Haven't you got Chopin's 'Dog Waltz', Tiphanie? That might make him move.'

'*Hark, hark, the dogs do bark*,' murmured Zoe.

'What about that one of Schubert's

about the lark? He might come in for a bird,' said Jack.

'I told you *not* to play Connections.' Tiphanie drew her head in from the window and threw a cushion at Jack to relieve her frustration. Only to let out a howl of rage when the cushion burst.

Barbara Streisand faded and Elgar's 'Pomp and Circumstance' took her place. The twins couldn't resist changing the words to 'Land of Hope and Feathers' as Tiphanie chased them round, throwing handfuls of feathers at them.

Throwing them didn't give her much satisfaction, though, so she grabbed another cushion and hurled it with all her might.

Jack ducked, but it still landed with a satisfying thud and burst just as the first one had done.

This time, it burst all over the angry personage of Kyle Cooper.

'Have you no consideration for other people?' Though muffled by feathers, his voice was harsh and full of the sarcasm Tiphanie had come to expect from him.

'There's a good connection,' Tiphanie told the twins, who were standing rooted to the spot, staring at the tall, frightening figure in the open doorway. 'Mr Sarky spitting feathers.'

'Or the *big bad wolf* in person,' whispered Zoe, watching in fascination as Kyle tried to shake himself free of the feathers.

'I suppose it is asking too much expecting you to respect the peace and quiet one normally has here. You'd never stop to think how loud music carries across water on a calm day, would you?'

'I can't think what's calm about today,' flashed Tiphanie, watching Kyle stride over and turn off her CD player. 'And I suppose it is asking too much for you to knock?' she stormed, goaded on by his palpable anger. 'This is the second time you've just walked in as if you owned the place.'

'As a matter of fact, I do own it,' he

drawled. 'However, I'd like to point out, just for the record, that I did knock on both occasions. And on both occasions you, Ms Timpson, were too occupied with other matters to hear.'

His eyes moved in the insolent way he had; Tiphanie knew he was remembering her clutching her unzipped jeans when he'd walked in on her and Tristan.

Then, an image of Kyle wearing his brief shorts flickered into her mind. 'I see you're fully dressed now.'

The words had popped out unexpectedly. Why did she have to recall the way he'd looked earlier? The way she'd felt? The same heat was surging through her body again now, and she wriggled uncomfortably.

'I'm dressed because I was settling down to work.' His voice was quiet but nonetheless dangerous for its quietness. 'And for my work,' he continued, 'I need peace and quiet. Lohengrin completely destroyed my concentration.'

To say nothing of how this orange-haired, fiery, beautiful woman is preventing me from concentrating. I really ought to know better than to be attracted to fiery and beautiful, he reminded himself. *I've been there, done that and suffered the heartache.*

He hated how his thoughts so often dwelt on his beautiful-on-the-outside-only ex-wife who'd flitted from man to man.

* * *

Watching him, Tiphanie saw the momentary shadows in his eyes and wondered. But he'd started moving towards her . . .

'And as for 'Big Bad Wolf' . . . ' He looked for a moment as if he were going to take her by the shoulders and shake her.

I want him to touch me, Tiphanie realised, and was filled with a sense of despair as his hands dropped to his sides. He muttered, 'I'll never finish the story I was writing now . . . it's fatal having to break off in full flow.'

'Typical writer's temperament,' mocked Tiphanie. 'You're all the same: selfish, self-centred, egotistical — '

'You seem to be an authority on writers,' he interrupted, his tongue heavy with obvious sarcasm.

'I should be. I've lived with two.'

'Ah, yes. Howard and Tristan.' He looked down at Tiphanie as if she were a nasty smell.

She'd been referring to her father and Tristan, but sheer perversity prevented her from enlightening him. And anyway, Zoe was tugging anxiously at her arm. 'Look, Mum — '

'What have I told you about that?' demanded Tiphanie, taking her anger out on Zoe. 'Don't call — '

Zoe cut off the words impatiently, 'Sorry, Tiphanie, but look. Crystal has moved to one of the open windows. Oh, now she's making strange growling noises. I think she's ordering Marmaduke to come in.'

'Either that, or she's about to join him out there. Keep still, everybody, and don't speak,' begged Tiphanie, tiptoeing over to Crystal and moving her along a bit.

'That's it, Crystal, keep swearing loud enough for Duke to hear you. That's it, good girl. He's creeping towards the window now . . . '

Moving slowly, Tiphanie knelt on the window seat and wriggled her top half out of the window.

She sensed Kyle's eyes on her back and was vaguely aware of his intake of breath, but most of her concentration was on her cat.

'Got you,' she said. Wriggling herself back in, Tiphanie closed the window, gestured to Jack to close the other two, and dropped a kiss on Crystal's head as she turned, with Marmaduke nestling in her arms.

'I don't believe this.' Kyle's voice was husky now, and his face seemed drained of colour as he ran his fingers through his dark shock of hair. 'There are two of them.'

Of course, Tiphanie realised, both cats had been eating in the kitchen when Kyle had come in yesterday. 'Don't worry.' Tiphanie was holding Marmaduke vertically against her; walking mischievously towards Kyle, she peered up at him. 'Don't worry. I know you don't like cats. I'll make sure they don't come tripping across the bridge to your cottage.'

Tiphanie didn't get the response she was expecting. The silence was almost painful. Kyle's eyes were fastened on the window as if he was mesmerised by something. But he looked away when Jack broke the silence.

'Tiphanie, what a connection I could make.'

'Mr Sarky doesn't look like the angry troll now,' said Zoe. 'I'm not being rude,' she explained, looking up at him, her eyes full of laughter. 'It's a game we play. We call it Connections, and tripping across the bridge connects with the story called *Three Billy Goats Gruff*. There's an angry troll in the story, and — '

'You're all crazy,' Kyle ground out. 'Just how long are you intending to stay here?'

'The twins — ' began Tiphanie, then she broke off and started again: 'I'm sorry, I haven't introduced you, have I? Zoe, Jack, this is Mr Cooper.'

'I thought you said his name was Mr Sarky?' Zoe smiled politely and held out a hand. 'How do you do, Mr Cooper? I do apologise for calling you by the wrong name before. I must have misheard Tiphanie. We're staying all week,' she concluded.

Tiphanie didn't miss the deepening of Kyle's scowl on receiving Zoe's information. 'Yes,' she confirmed. 'The twins are staying a week, and then they're going back to their gran's. But I . . . I'm staying as long as Tristan wants me.'

She also noticed how pale he looked,

and put it down to reined-in anger. 'And, of course, my cat will be staying too. Tristan's a real softie where cats are concerned.' Her expression was challenging as she met Kyle's eyes.

Eyes like deep, dark pools, drawing her in to drown.

'Yes, he must be.'

Tiphanie flinched at the steely tone. She knew exactly what Kyle meant to imply by his reply. He'd as good as called her a cat. He'd accepted her challenge and turned it against her.

She wished everything could be different; she didn't want his scorn. She wanted to see those brown eyes filled with tenderness. Her heart banged painfully, mourning at the impression Kyle had of her. An impression she'd done little to correct and a lot to strengthen, she acknowledged sadly to herself.

'Well, we mustn't keep you from your work any longer,' she said. She wanted him to go, wanted to be rid of the maelstrom within. Her heart felt heavy with pain and lies, her sorrow rising like a phoenix to mock her.

She didn't want him to see what she was feeling; she bit hard on her lip, trying to control her emotions. Then, dragging her gaze away from his, she stepped past him and held the door wide open.

He was breathing deeply as though fighting his own battle within himself. He obviously won, for there was no sign of breathlessness as he said coldly, 'I hope in future you'll remember about my work and keep the volume of your music down. That reminds me . . . Have you got my Maddy Prior disc with you? You didn't leave it with the hotel receptionist.'

'I had other things on my mind,' she told him. 'But, as you can see — ' She put Marmaduke down and gestured to the table beneath one of the windows. ' — I did bring my tapes and my discs with me. I'm sure yours is amongst them. I'll have a look.'

She started to move swiftly, still

anxious for his departure.

That was when she realised that feathers on an uncarpeted floor were slippery. But as she skidded forward, Kyle's hands shot out and grabbed her arms.

She felt a tingling in the pit of her stomach, her heart jolted and she felt the pulse in her neck pounding as she stared at his hands tightly clasping her arms.

Then she felt him take a deep breath and sensed *his* confusion. She sneaked an upward look through her eyelashes and saw his Adam's apple moving in his throat. Heat rippled under her skin, and she tried, in vain, to hold back a tiny murmur.

With a muttered exclamation, he loosened his grip and let go of her arms.

Now she felt bereft. She wanted his hands back on her arms . . . or better still, around her waist, pulling her close to him. She needed the relief only his touch would bring.

Ironically, the only touches Tiphanie felt were that of Crystal winding between her ankles and then Jack's fingers on her leg, as with a murmured, 'Come on, Mum, it's time to eat,' he picked the cat up.

Not trusting herself to speak just yet because her mouth was dry, Tiphanie didn't remind Jack he should be saying 'Crystal' and not 'Mum'. Besides, try as she might, she seemed unable to take her eyes off the hollow in Kyle's neck, and was once again thinking how she'd love to taste . . .

'Don't bother about the disc, Ms Timpson; I'll collect it some other time.' His voice sounded harsh, as though it was hurting him to speak. His tongue flicked out to moisten his lips; she imagined those lips on hers, imagined touching that tiny scar at the side of his mouth and feeling its texture on her tongue.

She inhaled so deeply her face jerked upwards, and she saw his expression of disgust.

Disgust for her or for himself? She didn't know, couldn't tell.

Whatever, it didn't quite hide the flame of desire that made his eyes sparkle like jet.

Awareness spiralled through her once more; and, trembling, she watched him turn and walk out of the door, leaving behind him air vibrant with electricity and a lingering scent that was his and his alone.

'Don't forget to knock when you come to collect your CD, and then wait until you're invited in!' she yelled, and she knew she was screaming out a protest.

A protest at him going and leaving her alone with overheated emotions.

Jack whistled a few recognisable notes from Handel's *Music for the Royal Fireworks*. Feeling as if she were fizzing like a firework herself, Tiphanie grated: 'Get these feathers cleared up, or both of you will feel the connection of my hand on a part of your body.'

The twins grinned; they were quite

used to her fiery temper, and she was aware they knew she'd never raise a hand to them.

Then, calming down slightly she said, 'I'll go down and make some waffles for breakfast.'

'You can get angry every morning if you end up making waffles to show us how sorry you are,' called Zoe to her aunt's departing back.

'We'll send for Mr Cooper to help you get angry,' added Jack.

'It's not anger I feel when he's around,' muttered Tiphanie a few minutes later, as she broke eggs into a bowl. 'It's pure and simple yearning . . . and I'm acting like a teenager,' she added furiously.

But she knew her body was far more aware than that of a teenager's. Knew that at last the thoughts of what could have happened on that lonely Fenland road three years ago, which had frozen all emotional feelings other than fear, had stopped haunting her.

Her body had been awakened. And

she wondered how she was going to cope with these feelings. Cope with seeing Kyle, cope with wanting to be loved by him.

That was nonsense. She beat the eggs hard. Love didn't enter into it. If anything, she despised the man. Hated him for making her body behave so uncontrollably. Detested him for thinking she allowed other men to make love to her.

Why didn't he know she'd been waiting for him all her life?

That last thought stunned her. Her hand froze on the whisk and she stared unseeingly out of the kitchen window. No. It isn't true; I won't let it be true.

4

Tiphanie's unhappy discovery made her feel restless. At what point in their stormy relationship had her feelings for Kyle changed?

Not that you can call it a relationship, she mused, dishing up a second helping of waffles for the twins. More like a series of unfortunate meetings. Why did he look as if he wanted to kiss me that day? Especially when he thought I'd spent the night with Howard. Did he feel he had to prove his own prowess?

She shook her head at that thought; nobody with such palpable potent masculinity would feel he had to prove anything, either to himself or to anyone else. Maybe anger turns him on, and I was angry when he wouldn't move to let me get into my room.

Tiphanie closed her eyes; she could

see the expression on his face, felt again the quivering awareness she'd felt at the time. But then he must have noticed I was upset, and . . .

'Tiphanie, can't you hear the phone? Do you want me to answer it?' Jack's voice broke into her memories, and she realised from his tone that it wasn't the first time he'd asked the question.

'Phone? Oh, yes, phone,' she said, glancing round for her mobile, and then realising the ringing was from Tristan's phone in the lounge.

'I guess you're lost in cartoon land, so I'd better go and answer it.' Jack gave an exaggerated sigh and got up from the kitchen table.

Not exactly, Tiphanie replied silently, quickly returning to that other place as, in her mind, she felt Kyle brushing her cheek with his thumb.

Zoe obviously thought the same as her twin, because she said loudly, 'Earth to Tiphanie! I asked if you're going to draw the Frolic family eating waffles?'

Before Zoe's question registered properly, Jack shouted from the lounge, 'Tiphanie! It's for you. Somebody called Natasha.'

Natasha was her editor, and hearing her name brought Tiphanie fully back to here and now. She turned off the gas jet and pushed the waffle pan to one side before calling, 'Ask her to hang on a minute, Jack. I'll take her call in the studio.'

Natasha knew she was taking a few days off to look after Jack and Zoe. Unsure of mobile phone reception on the salt marshes, Tiphanie had given her Tristan's landline number. But, even so, Tiphanie didn't want Natasha to hear the twins chatting in the background during what surely would be a conversation to do with work.

Though as she hurried up the twisty stairs, Tiphanie couldn't think why Natasha was phoning. They'd only spoken a few days ago and Natasha had said they were way ahead with episodes for the *Fenland Frolics*.

Tiphanie knew her mouth was stretched into a large smile when she went back into the kitchen. 'Great news,' she told Jack and Zoe. 'The *Fenland Frolics* are going to have a whole magazine to themselves. A Christmas Special with sixty-four pages.'

And that would keep her so busy she wouldn't have time to think of anything else. There wasn't much time at all for all the stages the magazine would need to go through before publication, so she'd have to work quickly.

'You can use the waffle story,' said Zoe. 'The one you were thinking of when the phone rang.'

That wasn't what she'd been thinking about at all. But now she'd really have to get Kyle-Mr-Sarky-Cooper out of her mind. Walking always helped to clear unwanted thoughts. 'We'll go for a long walk,' she said. 'The cats can come with us.'

'Haven't you noticed the weather's changed?' Jack asked. 'It's pouring with rain.'

'It might have stopped by the time we've done the washing-up,' replied Tiphanie, holding up crossed fingers.

'Can't you see there's no crockery or anything on the table? I washed the pots while you were in the studio on the phone,' Zoe said. 'Honestly, you've been acting really weird since Mr Cooper's visit.'

'It wasn't exactly a visit, Zoe. More like a visitation.'

Jack chuckled. 'He was rather angry, wasn't he?'

'He was at first, but I think he felt kind of scared when you leant out of the window, Tiphanie,' Zoe told her. 'I heard him catch his breath.'

'Let's not waste time talking about him. Put your cagoules and boots on, and we'll go for a walk, even though it's raining.'

Honestly, it was bad enough her own thoughts were taken up by that man

— she didn't want the twins to keep discussing him. A walk in the rain would give them all something else to think and talk about.

⋆ ⋆ ⋆

'It's a good thing we decided to leave the cats at home.' Jack looked up at Tiphanie, rivulets streaming down his face. They'd been walking for half an hour and it was raining harder than ever.

'It is,' Tiphanie agreed. 'I don't think this was one of my brightest ideas.'

The walk hadn't even served to take her mind off Kyle. She'd spent the whole time wishing over and over again that Tristan had gone over to explain things to him on the day her zip had got stuck, or that she'd explained things herself when Kyle had questioned her earlier this morning.

And now, after replying to Jack, her thoughts continued to circle round and round: I could have told him this morning Tris is my brother, instead of which I encouraged him to go on thinking Tris and I are something entirely different. Why was I so stupid? I know why . . . it's the way he scowled when Zoe told him we were staying for a week.

He looked as if he didn't want us here, didn't want *me* here. I had to let him think that somebody wanted me, even if he didn't. But afterwards, when I slipped and he grabbed me, he felt something then, I'm sure he did. Even though he was annoyed. No, make that appalled for feeling it. I could almost smell his desire.

'Can you smell it, Tiphanie?' At first, she thought she'd spoken her last thoughts aloud, and she looked down at Zoe in horror. 'The salt,' said Zoe. 'The smell of salt from the saltings, it makes my nose itch. I can taste it in the rain, too. It's making me thirsty.'

'You mean you want to go back. Come on then, turn round.' Suddenly Tiphanie felt guilty. For her own selfish reasons she'd brought the twins out for a walk in terrible weather, and then spent the whole time wrapped up in her own thoughts.

'I'm sorry, you two. I'm not being very good company, am I?'

'No worries, Tiphanie,' said Jack. 'We know you've got stuff to think about. You must be dead excited about your Fenland Frolics magazine. It's lucky that Natasha person had Tristan's phone number.'

'How did she, though?' asked Zoe. 'Does she know Tris?'

'I gave Natasha his phone number a few days ago when I let her know I'd be here instead of on holiday in Scotland.'

'Aww, Tizz, did you have to cancel a holiday in Scotland to look after us?' asked Jack.

'Yes, but don't worry about it, it's probably a good thing really.' Fleetingly, Tiphanie thought about Howard, and felt nothing but relief. Relief they hadn't gone on holiday together, for then surely they would have made love. After all, she had thought herself in love with Howard. She knew now those feelings had been nothing compared to what she felt for Kyle.

But what exactly do I feel for Kyle? she wondered in despair. I know I'm attracted to him, know I burn at his touch . . . he only has to look at me and I turn to liquid fire inside. Apart from all that, the main feeling is anger. He's so sarcastic, so supercilious, he'd be so wrong for me. I can't be 'in like' with him — let alone love.

I can't really have been waiting all my life for that sort of aggravation. I'm vulnerable at the moment because of what Howard and Felicity did to me, and ready to latch on to anybody who pays me any attention. That's why I wanted him to kiss me, to hold me close. I would have forgotten all about him if I'd never seen him again after those times at Lanleigh. It's just unfortunate he happens to be Tristan's nearest neighbour.

I'm sick of thinking about him. I'm going to put him right out of my mind and get on with my life.

She glanced down at the twins. They looked like waifs — soaking wet waifs.

'Race you back to Tris's,' she said suddenly, and it was good to see them running off with shrieks of delight.

'Isn't that Tristan's car?' Zoe asked a few minutes later, skidding to a halt and peering ahead through the pouring rain.

'Looks like it,' Tiphanie replied breathlessly. 'He should be on the train now, well on his way to Newcastle or wherever it is he's going. He was leaving his car at the station and hiring another one up there.'

She clutched at her side; running had given her a stitch. 'I hope he's got the percolator going, I could do with a coffee.'

'We'll run on and make sure he has,' offered Zoe. 'You know, Tiphanie, you're not very fit. You're puffing like that old steam train Gran took us on once. You'll have to take up jogging or something.'

Here I go again, Tiphanie fumed as, instead of seeing the twins running off, her mind conjured up an image of Kyle jogging along the river bank. Why does everything come back to him? She shook her head to try and rid herself of the image.

When she rubbed the dripping water out of her eyes she saw someone getting out of Tristan's car. Even though the weather made it hard to see clearly, she could tell it certainly wasn't her brother.

Anxious about the twins facing a stranger, she started to run again. Apprehension flickered through her as she wondered if this man had come to tell her something had happened to Tris.

★   ★   ★

'Tiphanie. How are you? It must be a year since I've seen you.' The sodden figure hurried towards her; he wasn't wearing a coat, and his clothes were plastered to his body. Tiphanie laughed up at Dave, an old school friend of Tristan's, as he explained. 'I met Tristan in the station car park hours ago — or, to be more exact, he fell over my feet as I lay under my car.'

They were walking back towards Marsh View now and the twins were waiting impatiently by the door. 'Something drastic happened to my car,' Dave continued, 'I'm not sure what. Luckily, Tris gave me his spare keys, and said I could use his if I couldn't get mine to go. Which, needless to say, I couldn't. On my way here, Tris's car got a puncture, and it took me ages to put the spare wheel on.'

'You're soaking wet and filthy dirty,' observed Tiphanie. 'Why on earth didn't you go straight home? Do you still live in the same place? It can't be far from here.'

'I thought I'd come and tell you about Tris lending me his car, in case you saw me in it and wondered what was going on. He told me you were staying here.'

'Pull the other one, Dave. What else has happened? You always were accident-prone.' Tiphanie pulled the big door key out of her pocket and unlocked the door. 'Straight through into the kitchen,' she ordered everyone. 'We can't drip in the lounge.'

While she and the twins got out of their soaking cagoules, Dave answered the question. 'To tell you the truth, I did something stupid. I locked my keys inside my car, and Kay won't be home from work until four o'clock. I thought you might take pity on me and let me have a shower here. I think I lay on some glass when I changed the wheel on Tristan's car. My back is prickling ominously.'

'Show him up to the bathroom, Jack, while I make a drink,' said Tiphanie. 'Root around in Tristan's room and see if you can find Dave some jeans and a sweater. They'll be huge on him, but at least they'll be dry.'

'If Jack and I change into old clothes, can we go and explore the basement room?' asked Zoe, as Tiphanie spooned coffee into the percolator. 'We're thinking of clearing it out and turning it into a den. The steps are quite safe, I asked Tristan last night. He said if we pile all the rubbish in a heap on that bit of rough ground before you get to the gate, he'll have a bonfire when he comes home.'

'You'll get soaking wet, carting rubbish over there.'

'It's stopped raining now,' said Zoe. 'Well, it's — ' She sneezed before she could finish and then rubbed her nose. 'I said the salt smell had made it itch. The rain has almost stopped,' she carried on. 'So can we go and explore the basement?'

'I suppose it will keep you both occupied,' said Tiphanie, by way of agreeing. 'But you'd better let me check anything that isn't just cardboard boxes or old newspapers before you dump it.'

Half an hour later, when Tiphanie was making sandwiches in the kitchen, Dave wandered in with a towel firmly tied around his lower half. 'I'm sure there *is* some glass in my back,' he told her. 'High up on the left-hand side. Will you have a look?'

He turned his back to her and she could see a red weal below his shoulder blade. 'You'd better sit down, I'll be able to reach it more easily then.'

'You always were a pint-size.' Dave chuckled. 'Do you remember how mad you used to get when we were kids and we called you that?'

'I do. I also remember that you were always doing something stupid then, as well. Like going out in the pouring rain without a coat. There is a sliver of glass here; it wouldn't have got through a coat. I'll get the first-aid box.'

'I did have a coat when I left home this morning,' he said when she returned. But — '

'Don't tell me. You locked it inside your car. Now, sit still while I try and dig this glass out.'

Tiphanie had removed the glass, put antiseptic on the wound, and was just sticking a plaster over it when there was a loud knock at the door. 'That'll be the twins with a pile of rubbish for me to check,' she said, hurrying out of the kitchen and into the lounge to open the door.

'Obeying orders and waiting until I'm invited in,' drawled Kyle. 'I noticed that Tristan was back and came to see if there's any mail for me. We take it in turns to collect it from the post office,' he explained.

'It isn't Tristan.' Tiphanie felt flustered as her body reacted to Kyle's nearness. 'He's gone away for a few days. Didn't he tell you he was going?'

'I'll go and get dressed, Tiphanie. Then I'll help Jack and Zoe with the stuff for the bonfire.' Dave's voice came from behind her and she guessed he was on his way to the twisty stairs. She tried to pull the door to, but she could tell from the expression on Kyle's face that he'd seen Dave's towel-clad figure.

'You don't waste much time, do you, Ms Timpson? You went from one man at the Festival to Tristan; and as soon as he's gone, there's another one on the scene. Are you trying to get into the Guinness Book of World Records?' His tone was blistering — his eyes blazing, and it seemed as if they were burning into her very soul.

'Kyle. Wait. I can explain. It's not what you think. None of it is.' But he'd already turned on his heel and was striding away.

Anger and hurt fought inside her. Why couldn't he have stopped to listen? 'Because he's arrogant and supercilious; he's nothing but an ignorant *skunk*, and I couldn't care less what he thinks of me,' she muttered and she slammed the door before marching back into the kitchen to tidy away the first-aid stuff.

'Who was that at the door?' Dave asked when he returned fully-dressed in his borrowed clothes. 'If I'd realised it wasn't the twins, I'd have stayed put. I tell you what, Tiphanie. I wouldn't like to cross that chap in a hurry. He looked absolutely livid when he caught sight of me.'

Tiphanie shrugged, fighting back tears. 'Him? Oh, he's nobody important,' she said, and the lie made a bitter taste at the back of her throat. 'Go and fetch the twins for me, Dave, while I finish making the sandwiches. They must be starving by now.'

Which is more than I am, she told herself dismally. I feel sick when I think of the way Kyle spoke to me, the way he looked at me. She wondered if he'd be watching to see when Dave left — and if he'd come over again.

But although Dave made plenty of noise when he left, revving up Tristan's car in a way that would have caused Tristan to cringe had he heard it, there was no sign of Kyle either then or later.

Maybe I really have seen the last of him, Tiphanie thought that night as she got ready for bed. Better that way, really. I'll be able to concentrate on *Fenland Frolics*, and on giving Zoe and Jack a good time.

★   ★   ★

It rained steadily without stopping for the next two days. The weather didn't bother the twins much, though; they were enthralled with their basement den. They'd found an old piano down there and although it was out of tune they clearly took great delight in trying to play something recognisable on it. They stayed down there for hours at a time, enabling Tiphanie to concentrate on her work.

Tiphanie was glad to have this unexpected time to spend at her drawing board. Although, as a freelance, she always had a good deal of commissioned work from various publishers — drawing zany pictures to illustrate someone else's stories or lettering the captions for comic strips — it was her own *Fenland Frolics* cartoons that were gaining her a popular following. Hence the editor's decision to publish the Christmas Special. By burying herself in her work, Tiphanie should have had less time to think about the disturbing presence in the cottage on the other side of the river.

But thoughts of Kyle continued to intrude. He appeared in her dreams, interrupting her sleep, and those dreams lingered tauntingly in her mind. And how was it that the atmospheric music she played to work to — soft, gentle pieces like Debussy's 'Clair de Lune' and his Preludes for when she was shading, or powerful tunes with a strong beat such as Rossini's *William Tell* Overture for when she was drawing bold outlines or action lines — all brought Kyle to mind? She carefully refrained from playing his Maddy Prior; neither did she play *Lohengrin* or Barbara Streisand.

To make matters worse, the twins seemed to be thinking about him as well. When she packed a picnic tea in a basket and took it down to the den, Jack was picking out a piano piece from *Children's Corner*.

'Debussy dedicated this to his daughter,' Jack informed her. 'I think I'll dedicate it to Mr Cooper. It's called 'The Snow is Dancing'. It reminds me of that day you threw a cushion at him, Tiphanie, and he had to clear all the whirling feathers from his face.'

'I didn't throw the cushion at *him*,' Tiphanie defended herself. 'He just happened to be there at the wrong moment.' He has a habit of that, she added silently as she plonked the basket down on top of a pile of books.

'I think he's really handsome,' Zoe said, sighing dramatically. 'You ought to make your character Freya Frolic fall in love with someone like him. I love the episodes where she's suffering from a broken heart. You know, Tiphanie, where you always draw her looking sad and wistful and have her cat doing something silly to try and cheer her up.

'Oh, that reminds me,' Zoe added, 'I found some sheet music in the piano stool. One of the songs would be great for you to listen to while you're doing a sad Freya picture. It's called 'My Coloring Book'. The chorus lines are about eyes watching her loved one walk away, colour them grey. And a heart who thought he'd be true so colour it blue . . . '

Tiphanie knew the song; she'd got the Kristin Chenoweth album *Coming Home*, and it was on that. To her dismay, right now, she empathised all too easily with the words. She didn't want to hear the part about arms being empty; it reminded her of when she'd held on to Kyle when she'd skidded on the feathers, and how bereft she'd felt when he'd let go of her arms. She wanted to tell Zoe to stop. But she couldn't speak, and Zoe continued in a gentle voice until she reached the end of the chorus: ' 'Colour him gone'.'

Zoe handed Tiphanie the sheet music and asked, 'Don't you think they're good words? You could draw Freya with a picture in a bubble above her head. A picture of a pirate, 'cos that's what Mr Cooper reminds me of. A pirate brave and bold and sort of dangerous-looking.'

'That's not a bad idea of Zo's,' Jack said. 'The pirate bit, not the soppy broken-hearted bit. I mean, can you imagine anyone ever feeling like the words in that song? Saying to colour the room they walk and sleep in *lonely*. It's stupid. There's no such colour as lonely.'

Oh, but there is, Tiphanie thought painfully. The song says it all, and whoever wrote it knew a thing or two. 'Colour it lonely' describes everything around me. Then, telling herself to stop being such an angsty drama queen, she pointed to the basket and — knowing reminding the twins about food would stop them talking about other things — said aloud, 'Aren't you going to bother eating this picnic I've made?'

'You go and get on with the *Fenland*

Frolics if you like,' said Zoe. 'We'll bring the basket back up to the kitchen later. It all looks *delish*,' she added, starting to unpack the food.

'Are you sure you don't want to go out somewhere after you've eaten? We could go for a walk, or a ride in the car.'

'We can find plenty to do down here, can't we, Zo?' Jack said.

Zoe nodded. 'It wouldn't be much fun walking or sitting in a car in this rain,' she replied.

Nothing seems to be much fun any more, Tiphanie thought as she made her way up the basement steps. She paused at the top of them and gazed across the river. I wonder where he is, what he's doing. I haven't caught so much as a glimpse of him for two days. Maybe he's ill. Perhaps he's lying in bed with a fever and there's nobody to look after him.

'Rot,' she muttered crossly. 'He's not human enough to get ill. And even if he were, he wouldn't want me to look after him.' Still muttering, chiding herself for being a drama queen again, she turned her back on the river, deciding to go and do as Zoe had suggested and get on with the *Fenland Frolics*.

Once inside, Marmaduke and Crystal wound themselves in between her ankles and meowed in unison.

'OK, you two, you needn't sound so pathetic. We'll go into the kitchen, I'll feed you, and then you can come up to the studio and pose for me again.' She often thought her Marmaduke knew exactly what that meant. He was so good at it.

The kitchen needed a good tidy, she acknowledged, clearing a space to put the sheet music down so she could share out a tin of pilchards between the cats, and then laughing at their impatient yowls as they waited for her to put their dishes in front of them.

Once they were tucking in, she picked up the sheet music and walked into the lounge and to the twisty stairs. She'd take a break tomorrow, she decided, hurrying up to the studio. She'd give everywhere a good going-over, and then take the twins somewhere even if it was still raining.

And as for *this*, she thought, glancing down at the sheet music, it can go away out of sight. She pushed it into a cupboard and wandered over to the desk to look at the work she'd done so far. Amazingly, she felt pleased with it.

She was a strong critic of her work and wouldn't settle for anything other than her best. 'Maybe I work better when my heart is aching,' she mused as she studied the drawing of Marmaduke and Crystal. When she'd sketched them, they'd been playing on the table where she kept her CD player and discs. She'd captured their exact positions and expressions, and had drawn a vase to take the place of the CD player and a decorated Christmas tree in the background.

'This can be part of a story that takes place in Joseph Frolic's junk shop,' she decided aloud. She'd given this character his name after looking up the meaning and discovering it meant 'He shall add'.

After inserting a disc — one with children's nursery rhymes on for the nice jerky rhythm — she grabbed a pencil and a clean sheet of paper and worked furiously, getting her ideas down in rough form as quickly as possible. If her portrayal of the customer in the junk shop resembled Kyle Cooper, she wasn't aware of it . . . at least not until she added a heavy chain bracelet on one hairy wrist.

Then, sighing in exasperation, she rubbed the customer out and replaced him with an attractive lady wearing sparkly diamonds in her ears and on her fingers. 'Better, much better.' Tiphanie laughed and drew three tiny beating hearts in front of Joseph's face. 'He doesn't really fancy her. He's in love with the money he thinks she's got. I'll call this one 'For Love or Money?'.'

She worked well, no other thoughts hindering her progress until she changed the disc for one containing gentler music. But 'All in the April Evening' had her putting her pencil down, picking up the binoculars Tristan kept in the studio for bird-watching, and walking over to one of the windows.

She stared across at the cottage across the river. What was Kyle doing on *this* April evening? It wasn't late enough to be dark yet, though the rain cast gloomy shadows and there was a light glowing softly from one of the cottage windows.

It brought on her loneliness again; she wondered how she could feel this way about and yearn for someone who, in reality, she scarcely knew. Acknowledging that didn't prevent her from turning to gaze around the studio and recalling the morning Kyle had suddenly walked in.

Dreamily, she touched her arms where Kyle had taken hold of them to prevent her from falling. She could feel the warmth coursing through her again. But then she recalled his expression of distaste before he'd turned away and left; now the heat left her body to be replaced with that empty loneliness again.

She might have put the sheet music away out of sight, but the words of the song ran hauntingly through her mind. 'Colour it lonely' was such an apt description of the studio at this moment. It came as a welcome relief when she heard Jack and Zoe running up to the studio with plaintive demands for hot chocolate and biscuits.

* * *

After their pre-bedtime snack, the twins needed no persuasion to dump the crockery in the sink until morning before going back to the studio to look at some of the *Fenland Frolics* cartoons they hadn't yet seen.

'I like this one about Dizzy Lizzie Frolic and the windmill,' Zoe said, laughing as she pointed to one of the completed strips. 'The title's neat, too.

'Plain Sailing'. Did you get the idea for this one the other day when we saw Mum — I mean, Crystal — sitting on the ledge outside?'

'Yes. She — or, I suppose, Tristan — should take some credit: gave me the idea for the next one as well. I've not put the finishing touches to it yet, but I'm going to call it 'What's in a Name?'. Felix Frolic, the lucky one, wins first prize for renaming a train.'

'So you got the idea because Chrysanthemum's name has been changed.'

'I did,' Tiphanie agreed. 'And if you think carefully about changing the name of a train, it connects to something I thought we could do tomorrow.'

'Have you started a game of Connections, or do you mean what I think you mean?' asked Jack.

'Both, really,' Tiphanie replied.

'So are you going to take us to see Thomas the Tank Engine?'

'But how does that connect to a

name change, Jack?' Zoe asked, frowning.

'Don't you remember, Zo — when we were little and Grandad told us Thomas the Tank stories from memory, he kept changing Thomas to Tommy.'

'That isn't a very good connection,' protested Zoe. 'But that's OK if it means we're going to the Nene Valley Railway. Are we, Tiphanie? It's great there.'

'We are. I thought I'd call in at the publishers in Peterborough first to give Natasha the three stories that are finished, and then we'll go and see if Thomas is in residence. Even if he isn't, you enjoy looking round the engine sheds, don't you?'

'We do,' Jack and Zoe said together.

'It will be good even if it's still raining,' Jack added. 'And I'll connect our outing to James Bond.'

'I get that connection. Part of *Octopussy* was filmed there,' Zoe said. 'And, talking of James Bond films, I see a connection to one in this.' She pointed to the drawing Tiphanie had sketched for the start of the 'For Love or Money?' story.

'*Diamonds Are Forever*,' Jack said immediately.

'And,' Zoe continued, 'it sort of has a connection with Mr Cooper the pirate man.'

'I give up on that,' said Jack.

'That character who's always stroking his Persian cat is in it,' Zoe said. 'And the pirate man doesn't like cats.'

'I don't think that's one of your better connections, Zoe,' Tiphanie said, silently cursing her niece. 'But how about you connect to Wee Willie Winkie?'

'Are you children in your beds, because it's past eight o'clock?' said Jack. 'OK, Tiphanie, we'll go and get our pyjamas on.'

Tiphanie sighed as she watched them go out of the studio. Why had Zoe had to mention Kyle? Now she'd probably dream about him again tonight.

5

Tiphanie woke early, feeling refreshed and lively — probably because no dreams of Kyle had haunted her sleep after all. She was delighted to see the weather had changed and, without bothering to dress, hurried downstairs and opened the door for the cats. 'You'll have to stay inside later while we're out,' she told them. 'Go and have a nice stroll around.'

Half an hour later, she was enjoying her second cup of coffee and thinking about having a purge of the kitchen before the twins got up, when her peace and quiet was rudely interrupted by the sounds of a cat fight.

She dashed outside in time to see Marmaduke chase Crystal up the tree. 'There might only be the one tree here, but it sure causes a lot of trouble,' she mused. Then, to her horror, she saw that Crystal's collar had got caught on a branch. All her struggling and meowing only served to make matters worse. She was well and truly stuck, and likely to be choked or strangled any second.

Without stopping to think, Tiphanie swarmed up the tree. Having been brought up with three brothers, she found no difficulty in this feat. In no time at all, she reached Crystal and, speaking soothingly, managed to undo her collar.

All would have been well if a huge hairy Alsatian dog hadn't been taking a walk. Obviously catching sight of Marmaduke on the ground by the tree, the dog bounded forward with joyful barks. With one leap, Marmaduke joined Tiphanie and Crystal in the tree.

If there was one thing Tiphanie was wary of — apart from spiders, and she was downright scared of those — it was dogs. And this huge, hairy, barking monster of a dog seemed intent on jumping right into the tree with them. Trembling and whimpering and still clutching a hissing Crystal, Tiphanie climbed even higher.

Her one panicky idea was to get high enough so she could reach the ledge beneath the studio windows and bang on one, hoping Jack or Zoe would hear and open it so she could get in that way.

As she reached close to the window of the bedroom the twins were in, she saw their sleepy but surprised faces as they peered towards the tree.

'Go up and open the studio windows,' she yelled as she reached precariously towards a higher branch. Her voice enticed the dog to bark even harder, Crystal dug her claws into her arm and Tiphanie loosened her grip. The cat scrambled down to a branch below where Marmaduke was sitting. United now, the two cats hissed and yowled ferociously at the barking dog.

'Go and get the windows open,' Tiphanie yelled again at the twins.

⋆ ⋆ ⋆

On the other side of the river Kyle, who'd taken advantage of the weather to go for a jog, scowled in annoyance at the noise. Surely that woman hadn't got a dog as well? Changing his pace, he made for the bridge, ran quickly across it, and then increased his pace even more as the noise and his anger gathered momentum. It was too much having his peace and quiet destroyed like this by Ms Timpson and her menagerie.

The Alsatian, possibly aware of the anger emanating from the man pounding towards the tree, fled seconds before Kyle reached it. 'Good riddance, too,' muttered Kyle. But he tried to control his anger when he saw the worried expression on the face of the little girl standing by the tree.

'Oh, Mr Cooper, I was so glad when I saw you dashing over the bridge, I dashed even quicker down the twisty stairs and outside,' Zoe greeted him breathlessly. 'Tiphanie's almost at the top of the tree and she's going to try and jump across to the ledge so she can climb in one of the studio windows. I think it was to get out of the dog's way. She isn't too keen on dogs. You've got to stop her. Make her come down.'

Kyle stared upwards, and between the leafy branches caught sight of Tiphanie's bare legs. Only she would climb a tree in a shortie nightdress, he thought as he called aloud, 'Ms Timpson! Tiphanie, climb back down. The dog has gone.'

'Are you sure it's gone?' Her voice sounded faint and quavery. 'I don't think I can stretch my legs across to the ledge anyway.'

'It's gone and won't come back. Can you get down on your own, or shall I come up and help you?'

'You mustn't come up. You'll frighten the cats. I'll have to lift Crystal and carry her. I don't think she'll come down on her own. But it looks like Marmaduke is on his way down.' Tiphanie's voice was bordering on hysteria, and Kyle paused with his hands already on the nearest branch in preparation for swinging himself up.

'Don't climb up,' urged Jack, who'd joined them. 'If Marmaduke panics and freezes, Tiphanie's likely to do something really stupid, like trying to carry both cats. She'll be OK now the dog's gone. She's a brilliant climber and look, she's on her way down.'

'She's still a long way off the bottom. What the devil was she thinking of, climbing up so high. Can't *anyone* control her,' Kyle growled, peering anxiously up the tree.

'Tad can, but she doesn't see much of him any more. We don't, either. We live with our grandma most of the time because Mummy goes away a lot. Mummy says that's why she gets on so well with Tristan, because he doesn't try to control her,' Zoe said.

'I don't think Mr Cooper really expected an answer, Zo,' Jack said, before looking briefly at Kyle. 'You'll have to excuse her, Mr Cooper. She always babbles when she's nervous or worried.' But the boy's voice was hoarse, indicating he was also concerned by Tiphanie's descent.

'Look,' he said, seconds later. 'Here's Marmaduke. He's near enough for me to reach if you'll lift me up, Mr Cooper.'

'Eeeek,' Zoe said at the same time. 'Tiphanie almost missed her footing then.'

Kyle swiftly lifted Marmaduke down, handed him to Jack, and started to climb the tree. 'It's all right, Tiphanie,' he said softly. 'Marmaduke is safe, so just you take it slowly now.'

'Crystal weighs a ton, and if I try to put her down she digs her claws in — so I can't do anything but take it slowly, can I?'

Tiphanie's snappish retort alleviated Kyle's concern a little; in truth, his racing pulse had little to do with that. Her shortie nightdress had ridden up quite some way, and he stayed still, watching as she climbed slowly, branch by branch, towards him.

Whether it was Crystal digging her claws in or awareness of Kyle a way below her that caused her to slip, Tiphanie didn't know. But slip she did; somehow missing Kyle's outstretched hands and landing on the ground with a thump.

'Tiphanie . . . Mum . . . are you hurt?' screeched Zoe. Then Crystal, hissing and spitting, finally managed to break free of Tiphanie's arms, and Zoe knelt over Tiphanie's still form. 'Say something,' Zoe pleaded. But Tiphanie couldn't find the strength to reply.

'Move, Zo,' Jack said huskily. 'Let Mr Cooper have a look.'

Tiphanie knew she should reassure the twins she was all right, to tell them she was recovering from the trauma, but the firm but gentle hands exploring her body felt good and her intentions fled. Peeping through her half-closed eyes, she noted Kyle's anxious — almost tender — expression, and she allowed a small groan to escape.

Kyle must have realised the groan wasn't because she was hurting anywhere, for, in a second, his expression changed. He tugged at the hem of her nightie, pulling it down as far as it would go. *Not very far*, Tiphanie thought, suddenly embarrassed, as he tersely informed the twins: 'She'll live. It would take more than falling down a tree to damage a tough nut like her.'

Tiphanie sat up quickly. 'There wouldn't be any question of me damaging myself if you hadn't climbed the tree to ogle me when the whole length of my legs must have been on show.' This time her groan and the following faintness were genuine. She was vaguely aware of strong arms lifting her, vaguely aware of a strong heartbeat as she nestled her head against his comforting chest.

She thought he was taking her inside, and then for a while it was if she were floating up the twisty staircase. She heard the twins' anxious voices in the background and a husky reply from Kyle before she became aware of her body being lowered. The strong arms released her and she whimpered fretfully.

'Don't worry, you'll feel better soon. Just let me make you comfortable. That's it. Rest now, Tiphanie, everything will be all right.'

'Nice when you speak softly,' she murmured. 'You're like the gentle giant, not really gruff and grim. Not really Mr Sarky. Not . . . '

* * *

But her lids had closed over her smoky-grey eyes and she was drifting off into sleep. At least, Kyle thought it was sleep. Frowning, he wondered if he should send for a doctor. But her breathing seemed normal, as did her pulse. He allowed his fingers to linger a moment at the base of her throat.

'Will she be all right, Mr Cooper?' Zoe whispered. 'She didn't fall that far, she was near the bottom of the tree when she slipped.'

'She's OK,' Jack said. 'She just sat up too quickly to yell at Mr Cooper, Zo. Nobody could shout like she did and not be all right.'

'We'll let her rest for a while,' Kyle decided. 'Then we'll wake her up with a strong, sweet cup of tea. Are these animals allowed on the bed?' He pointed to Marmaduke and Crystal, who'd arranged themselves like sentinels on either side of Tiphanie.

'They're probably feeling a bit shaken up, too,' Zoe told him seriously. 'After all, it must have been them that horrible dog was barking at really. Besides, Mum will feel more secure being with both of them, and Tristan told me it's important for her to feel secure. He said the therapist told him that.'

'And Tiphanie will feel better if she wakes and sees them with her,' Jack added.

Kyle nodded. In spite of their

unconventional way of life, there was no doubt Jack and Zoe still cared deeply for Tiphanie; and, even if they occasionally forgot, didn't seem fazed by having to call her by her name instead of —

Zoe broke into his thoughts by saying plaintively that she was starving. 'We haven't had breakfast yet, Mr Cooper. Have you? 'Cos if you haven't, would you like me to make you some?'

His heart melted when he looked at the little girl with her hair and eyes so like Tiphanie's. 'The three of us will go and make some together,' he said.

$\star$ $\star$ $\star$

When Tiphanie woke it was almost dusk. The bedside lamp was on low and she could see a faint moon through the open curtains. 'I don't remember going to bed,' she muttered aloud, and then sat up curiously when she heard Zoe giggle.

'Take it easy. Don't move too quickly.'

That can't really be Kyle, not sounding so gentle and concerned — and certainly not in my bedroom,' Tiphanie thought yearningly.

'Can you remember what happened, Tiphanie?' Dark brown chocolate eyes, hawk-like features and a tiny scar at one corner of his mouth. If this was a dream it was very real; she could even smell his sea-breeze cologne. But how? And why? She had to stop drowning in those eyes. Slowly, she moved her gaze downwards, and as her glance fell on the two sleeping cats her memory flooded back.

'Did I hurt myself when you made me fall out of the tree?' she asked, looking at Kyle again. 'And why is it almost dark outside? How long have you been here? How long have I been here, and is Crystal all right? I was holding her when I fell. Tristan will kill me if she's hurt. It's your fault if she is, Kyle-Peeping-Tom-Cooper. Let me look at her.'

'Obviously you do remember what

happened.' He'd spoken in the familiar mocking tone, half-smiling at her before moving away.

'Mum — sorry, Tiphanie, Crystal is fine and so is Marmaduke and so are you.' Zoe flung herself into Tiphanie's arms. 'The doctor came to see you. He said you'd be all right, but I didn't believe him. We couldn't wake you up. You didn't even wake when Kyle — '

'Shush, Zoe. Let her collect her thoughts properly.' Gently, Kyle interrupted Zoe's flow of chatter. 'Move away now, sweetie, your brother's here with a snack for her.'

'Hi,' said Jack. 'Are you feeling better for your sleep? You've slept all day, you know. Kyle, Zo and I cleaned the kitchen up and then made a tree-house. Oops, maybe I shouldn't mention the tree.'

'We didn't leave you by yourself though,' said Zoe, snuggling next to her. 'We took it in turns to sit with you.'

'That's right,' said Jack. 'And when Zo said she thought you looked like you would wake soon, I went and made this for you. It's hot chocolate and some bread and butter. Kyle said you should have sweet tea, but I knew you wouldn't drink that.'

'Too right I wouldn't have.' Tiphanie reached gratefully for the mug of hot chocolate. 'How come you're both calling Mr Cooper 'Kyle' all of a sudden?' she asked between sips.

It was Kyle who answered that question. 'We've spent the whole day together,' he said. 'It seemed pointless to stand on ceremony. Besides, you're a fine one to talk about informality. Why do you encourage them to call you Tiphanie?'

She shrugged. 'Maybe it makes me feel more carefree. They are more formal sometimes, but I'm glad to say that isn't often. It's bad for my image and makes me feel old. It's strange, really . . . '

She nibbled thoughtfully at a slice of bread and butter. 'I was only seventeen when they were born. I used to love pushing them out in their twin pram because, somehow, it made me appear older. I used to like that *then*.'

'Daddy used to tease you about it, didn't he? I remember you telling us that once.'

'Yes, he did.' Tiphanie ruffled Zoe's hair, feeling sad as she thought about her brother and mother losing their lives in the plane crash. 'It's nice to hang on to happy memories, isn't it?' she said softly. She knew this little scene in the bedroom would find a place in her memories, too.

* * *

Watching her, Kyle had to force himself not to take her in his arms and hold her close. But, he reminded himself grimly, this vulnerable person isn't the real her. The real Tiphanie was the flighty one . . . the man-a-moment Tiphanie, who let the twins' grandmother look after them while she got on with her own life.

'Do you want to get up for a while?' he asked abruptly. 'I'll go down and prepare a light meal if you like. At least I can find my way round in the kitchen now we've tidied it up a bit.'

He hadn't really meant it as a criticism, but Tiphanie clearly thought he had because she flushed as she spoke. 'I know it was a mess, but I've spent the last two days working. I was going to begin cleaning up when the cats started fighting. Then the dog came, and then — '

Kyle interrupted with a terse, 'Food will be ready in twenty minutes. Come and help me, Jack. You stay with your . . . with Tiphanie, Zoe, in case she needs any help getting dressed.'

* * *

I guess that was his way of telling me not to go down in my nightshirt, Tiphanie thought, resenting his high-handed manner. He probably thinks I slop round in it and never do any work

141

at all. What a strange mixture he is. One minute he's soft and gentle, and the next he's Mr Sarky and high-handed and hard. I suppose I must have disrupted any plans he had for today, even though I couldn't do anything about that. Well, I suppose the sooner I get up and go down, the sooner he can go.

'You are all right, aren't you, Tiphanie?' Zoe wrinkled her brow as she watched her get out of bed. 'Your face is ever so red.'

'I . . . er . . . I wasn't wearing *this* nightie this morning. So how — ?'

'I looked in the drawers and found you a clean one. It was ever so hard getting your dirty one off and that one on with you so fast asleep. I had to ask for help in the end.'

'Who helped you?' Tiphanie's voice came out in a squeak, and she closed her eyes as she waited for an answer.

'Kyle . . . ' Zoe giggled.

Embarrassment flooding through her, Tiphanie sank onto the bed.

'Kyle asked the doctor to help me,' Zoe continued. 'He said you were annoyed enough because he'd seen too much of your legs. But that other nightie was ever so short. Kyle couldn't *help* seeing a lot of your legs when you climbed down the tree, could he?'

'I suppose not,' Tiphanie agreed; stretching out her legs, she was secretly glad she'd had a wax job a couple of weeks ago. At least Kyle had seen them at their best.

'Kyle stroked them,' Zoe said, as if she'd read Tiphanie's thoughts. 'When he saw me watching he said he was just making sure you hadn't hurt them when you fell out of the tree. But I think he was admiring them,' she added with another giggle. 'He had a sort of dreamy look in his eyes. Well, he did at first . . . Afterwards, his eyes turned all sort of cold and hard, if you know what I mean.'

'I know exactly what you mean,' Tiphanie replied bleakly. She'd seen that particular look all too often. It was her own doing that he'd got *some* wrong impressions, but not as many as he seemed to have.

Perhaps 'Mr Wrong' would be a better name for him than 'Mr Sarky'. What with that rat fink Howard who'd cheated on her, and Kyle-flipping-Cooper who loathed the person he thought she was, she certainly had the knack of falling for the wrong man, didn't she?

Not that Howard had ever caused such dizzying currents to surge through her just by thinking of him. And it isn't thinking of Kyle doing that now, she told herself, getting off the bed. It's hunger for food, not for him, making me feel like this.

6

A frisson of awareness darted through Tiphanie as she stood leaning against the arched doorway into the kitchen and watched Kyle. He was at the sink washing the dishes they'd used for their meal; he'd insisted on clearing up while she put the twins to bed. They were perfectly capable of getting themselves into bed; nevertheless, eager to escape the sweet intimacy that sitting at the table had engendered, she'd agreed thankfully to Kyle's suggestion.

But surely that intimacy had existed only in her mind? He'd been very quick to apologise and draw back his legs when his foot had touched hers under the table, and he hadn't spoken one unnecessary word to her. In fact, Jack and Zoe had dominated the conversation ... though occasionally she'd looked up and caught Kyle staring broodingly at her.

Now, her glance rested briefly on his hips and then on the taut outline of his buttocks — his jeans fitted him like a second skin and she had to fight her overwhelming need to be close to him. She wanted him to turn round and . . . No. She caught her breath painfully. If he turned round, he might guess what she was feeling.

As though sensing her presence — maybe he'd heard her shallow breathing — he raised his head. He didn't turn, his eyes locked on her reflection in the window over the sink.

★ ★ ★

He took in her petite appeal. She was wearing a high-necked, long-sleeved top, and the smooth outlines of her hips and legs were covered by pale green denim jeans belted at her tiny waist. It looked as if she'd purposely chosen clothes to hide her body but he knew what delight lay beneath. *A delight she's offered to too many*, he reminded himself harshly.

★   ★   ★

Tiphanie knew he was looking at her; all her nerve ends were tingling, her heart jolting, and her pulse racing. She was mesmerised by his hands moving rhythmically as he rinsed the plates then placed them in the rack, and his air of efficiency fascinated her. But she wanted to feel those hands on her again. No, that wouldn't be enough; she wanted to be crushed within his embrace.

She knew she should stop thinking like this, knew that this attraction could be perilous. But why didn't he speak when he clearly knew she was here? It was like they were suspended in time. No, it wasn't. If they were, she wouldn't be able to feel or think. And what was Kyle thinking? What was he feeling? Or, actually, maybe the two of them were talking without speaking.

For a nanosecond her thoughts went to the twins and the connection they'd come up with there. Like her, they loved the heavy metal band Disturbed, and David Draiman's haunting version of 'The Sound of Silence' where he sang of people talking without speaking.

But right now, Tiphanie couldn't bear this silence between her and Kyle; it was tearing her apart. Surely he'd finished the washing-up and would turn round and say something.

He didn't, though. So Tiphanie forced herself to speak.

'Kyle?' Her voice was husky and she cleared her throat. 'Kyle, I haven't thanked you yet for looking after me and the twins today. I hope it hasn't interfered too much with your workload. I know only too well how frustrated one gets when there's a deadline to meet.'

'Oh, yes,' he drawled, turning at last and eyeing her with a taut and derisive expression on his face. 'You told me you'd lived with two writers, so you should know.'

She wasn't sure if it was that expression or the way he'd spoken; but, goaded beyond all reason, she took a few steps forward, bent down, and picked up one of the double dishes that contained cat food and water. 'I'll wipe that supercilious look off your face,' she hissed, and flung the dish.

She looked round for something else to throw, but before she could move, Kyle strode forward and gripped her wrists none too gently. Fish and water dribbled down his face and his eyes blazed into hers.

'I know what it's like working to a deadline, because I have to do that myself,' she said. She tried to ignore the pressure of his hands around her wrists, but his firm clasp was creating havoc with what she wanted to say. When she opened her mouth to explain it was her brother Tristan and their father she'd lived with, the wrong words popped out. 'You smell of fish and you're hurting my wrists,' she told him, stamping hard on his foot.

His grip loosened, though he didn't release her wrists. Instead, he half-dragged her over to the sink. Then he let go, but only to place one of his hands on the back of her head whilst turning on the cold tap with the other. 'This should cool you down,' he grated, pushing her head under the flow and also using the water to clean the mess off his face.

She wriggled furiously against his thighs as she tried to get free. Kyle groaned and pulled her round towards him. Lowering his head he covered her lips with his own.

His mouth was surprisingly gentle, as though he were healing any hurt his previous actions and words had caused. His tongue touched her lips — soothingly, caressingly. She tried to hold back her response, but as if of their own volition her lips parted to offer him entry, and her mouth and tongue gloried in the warmth she found within his. His face was still wet, and the mingling dampness and warmth further kindled the flame inside her.

She pushed closer to him, her body awash with the most delicious sensual awareness. Then she felt his fiercely indrawn breath, felt the pressure of his lips ease. No, no, she protested silently, clinging to them.

'No.' He ground the single word out and pushed her away from him. Her spine met the edge of the draining board with a thud and she whimpered. She was aware of tears of pain and bewilderment streaming down her face as she looked up at him.

'Tiphanie. I didn't mean that to happen. I didn't mean to hurt you.' He reached for a towel and gently rubbed her hair, then his fingers feathered onto her face and beneath her eyes as they followed the tears. 'Don't cry. Please don't cry,' he whispered. 'Come on, let's get you sitting down.'

He led her into the lounge, lowered her into an armchair, and crouched down in front of her. 'Just try to relax,' he murmured. 'I'll go and pour you a brandy, I know Tristan has some. I think I could do with one, too.'

Her back wasn't hurting. Yes, it had jarred her for a moment when she'd banged it on the draining board, but her tears had been more for the way he'd said 'No' after he'd stopped kissing her and pushed her away. The memory of that warm velvet kiss still lingered — all the way down to her very soul. She wanted to beg him to take her back in his arms, but she fought for composure and said calmly, 'A small brandy sounds like a good idea.'

He touched her knee lightly as he rose and she shuddered, trying to control the darts of sensation that threatened to destroy her composure.

'Don't worry,' he said, obviously mistaking the reason for her shudder. 'I'm not going to take liberties again. You have my word on that.' His eyes looked almost black now and seemed full of loathing — but for which one of them, Tiphanie didn't know.

Neither do I care, she lied valiantly to herself as she watched him walk over to the drinks cabinet to pour the brandies. She didn't want him to touch her again. Being close to him just brought sorrow. She'd forget about what happened in the kitchen and act like it never happened.

Immediately forgetting that resolution, she recalled the time outside her room at Lanleigh when he'd *almost* kissed her. Then, the same as this time, he'd made her good and mad first by implying she was promiscuous. An implication she'd done little to deny. Suddenly she was filled with regret and self-loathing.

'It's not as bad as that. Drink it, it will do you good.'

Tiphanie had no recollection of taking the glass of brandy from Kyle, but at his words she realised she was holding it. She looked up and realised he was sitting in the armchair opposite hers. How long had he been there watching her?

'You've been glaring at it for five minutes,' he added, as if answering her unspoken question. 'That's no way to treat an excellent brandy like this.'

Obediently, she sipped from the glass. Now she was acutely aware of the lean sprawl of Kyle's legs, his fingers around his brandy glass, the hairs on his arms, the glinting of the heavy chain around his wrist.

OK, if he could act in such a relaxed manner, then so could she. 'You know, I can't understand how I slept so long.' There, a safe topic, she congratulated herself inwardly.

'The doctor said you were in an extremely deep sleep, but assured me it was a natural one, and it was your body's way of recovering from the fright you'd had. His only concern was that you might not remember what had happened. Have you always been scared of dogs, Tiphanie?'

'I've always been wary of them,

especially big, fierce-looking ones. Actually, I'm wary around small dogs, too, but I don't know why. I've never been bitten by one.'

They fell silent for a while as though a somewhat uneasy truce had been declared. Tiphanie wriggled restlessly. Kyle had finished his brandy; surely he'd soon be thinking of leaving? She didn't really know if she wanted him to go or not, he got her so mixed up inside. It was almost peaceful, though, the two of them sitting here like this. It was as if they'd only just met, or were starting over again.

'What were you lecturing on at Lanleigh?' he asked suddenly. 'Are you an author? I don't think I've seen your name on any books.'

'I'm a cartoonist. I illustrate other people's work, or do the lettering for captions. And I write and illustrate my own cartoon strips, too.' She went on to tell him about the *Fenland Frolics*. 'I think of them as my second family,' she said — and felt surprised at having admitted that to him. 'They appear every week in a woman's magazine, so you probably won't have seen them,' she concluded.

'From their name, I'm guessing they're slightly crazy and eccentric,' he said, raising one eyebrow questioningly. And when she nodded, he added, sounding genuinely interested, 'I'd like to see your cartoons. Is that what you've been working on since you've been here?'

'Yes. I was supposed to be on holiday . . . ' She broke off, remembering that Kyle knew about the holiday she'd meant to be going on with Howard. But Kyle made no comment, so she resumed. ' . . . then my editor phoned to tell me they wanted to produce a sixty-four page *Fenland Frolics* Christmas special. It's an extremely short deadline, so I had to get down to it straight away.'

'I'd really like to see some of your work,' he said again.

'Come up to the studio and I'll show

you what I've done for the special so far.'

'I don't suppose you could bring it down here to show me, could you?'

'What's wrong? Did it sound too much like 'Come upstairs and see my etchings'? You'll be perfectly safe. I'm not going to take liberties. You have my word on that.' She threw what he'd said to her earlier back at him.

'That all depends on what one thinks of as taking liberties.' The mocking tone was back in his voice and, for a moment, she thought they'd lost the camaraderie that had appeared to be growing between them.

'I suffer from height vertigo,' he said abruptly. 'I used to ride a motorbike. One night I skidded on ice and rode it into a wall. My pillion passenger was killed.' Shadows lurked in his eyes; his pain and unhappiness almost tangible. Tiphanie moved swiftly to his chair, knelt beside it and took his hand in silent sympathy.

He obviously couldn't bring himself

to talk about that part of the accident, for he continued, 'I got off lightly, really.' With his free hand he fingered the scar at the corner of his mouth. 'This was my only visible reminder after the medics had patched me up. However, my sense of balance was slightly impaired, and after a few unpleasant experiences of dizziness when I went up a ladder, I developed a real fear of heights.

'For a couple of years I tried to fight it. I stayed living here in Marsh View. But if I went up to the studio . . . ' He shrugged. 'Anyway, when the cottage on the other side of the river was put on the market, I bought it and moved in. I couldn't bear the thought of parting with my old smock mill, though, so I decided to rent it out.'

Tiphanie felt sure Kyle hadn't come to terms with the death of his pillion passenger, and she wanted to try and help him do so. Even though she'd had no involvement in the accident that had cost her brother and mother their lives, she knew only too well how it hurt facing up to the death of someone close. She also knew this wasn't the right time. 'But you went up to the studio the other day,' she said instead.

'Anger at the noise you were making overcame my fear for a while.'

Zoe had picked up on his fear, recalled Tiphanie. She said he looked scared when I leant out of the studio window. Me doing that probably brought his height vertigo on.

'But today you were going to climb the tree to help me down. And you carried me up to my bedroom afterwards.'

'You sound like a goat with all your 'but's.' A smile ruffled his mouth and she suddenly felt a new closeness between them. 'I think worry for you was the uppermost thought in my mind. Though I wasn't tested too much; the branch I was on wasn't that far off the ground. As for carrying you to your room — concentrating on not jolting you got me through.'

'But what about the tree-house Jack and Zoe said you built?'

'I made sure it wasn't far up. I told them it was for their safety when really I was thinking of myself. Deep down, I'm a wuss.'

'That's rubbish,' Tiphanie scoffed. 'I bet you'd have climbed right to the top of the tree if I'd needed you to. And at least you've got a reason for your fear. It's not like my fear of dogs.'

'There'll be a reason for that somewhere.' Kyle stroked her hand lightly. 'It's been good sharing hang-ups, but that's enough of morbid talk for now. Time you went up to get your 'etchings'.'

He'd spoken teasingly, and Tiphanie gloried in the almost tangible warmth that seemed to surround them. A hint of sadness still lingered in his eyes, though. Guessing he wanted a few minutes alone, Tiphanie rose reluctantly.

She frowned and stood still for a moment. 'Did I hear a car outside? No,

I couldn't have done.' She glanced at the wall clock. 'It's half past ten. Nobody would come calling so late.'

But they heard a car door slam, saw a figure lit by moonlight hurry past the window, and then there was a loud hammering on the door.

'I'll go.' Kyle jumped up from his chair; his long legs covered the distance in no time at all, and he flung the door open.

Tiphanie stood on tiptoe to peer over his arm. To her horror, Howard was standing on the top step.

'So *he* is the real reason you cancelled our holiday,' Howard snarled and glared at Kyle, who'd stepped to one side, before turning his stare on to Tiphanie. 'I finally managed to get the address and Tristan's landline number from that Madge woman who was at your house. But I wanted to speak to you face-to-face, not on the phone. I've been driving around for hours trying to find this place.

'I was prepared to find you with

Tristan, I could have handled that. I should be able to, it's happened often enough before. Last time, if you remember, I found the two of you in a hotel.'

Tiphanie remembered all right. She'd cancelled a lunchtime date with Howard because Tristan had needed to talk to her about something. She'd gone to the hotel where Tris had been staying, and Howard had happened to see them having lunch in the hotel's restaurant. He'd almost, though not quite, caused a scene then — but that was nothing compared to his anger now. He was clearly working himself up to say more.

Would it make things better or worse to protest, to try and explain? wondered Tiphanie. Not that Howard merited any explanation — and after what he'd got up to with Felicity, how dare he imply she'd come here to be with Kyle?

And Kyle, how was he taking this onslaught? Should she tell him her true relationship with Tristan right now?

She'd been meaning to anyway. She glanced sideways at him and went cold at the tight, grim look on his face, the hardness in his eyes.

She'd left it too late to speak anyway; Howard had taken a deep, harsh breath, clearly ready to go on. 'I came here prepared to forgive you for letting me down once again, Tiphanie, for putting Tristan's needs before mine once again. But to find you here with someone you met for the first time a few days ago at Lanleigh . . . Well, that's it, Tiphanie. For once and all, we're through. It's finished. Do you hear me? Finished. It's over.'

Turning, Howard leapt down the four steps and marched over to his car. He flung himself into it and drove off with a screeching of tyres.

'It was over anyway,' Tiphanie said as Kyle turned towards her. 'And what Howard said about Tristan, it isn't what it seems. Tristan is — '

'I'm not interested in your complicated love life.' Kyle stared coldly down at her. 'Or in any of your life,' he added, stepping out. 'I'd lock the door behind me if I were you, Tiphanie. Though I'm not you. You'll probably leave it wide open. An open invitation for any passing man,' he stressed before going down the steps and striding away.

Tiphanie was lost for words. She was hurting too much to speak. There was no way she could call Kyle back. She doubted he'd come anyway, she thought, as she watched him make his way towards the bridge. An acute sense of loss filled her very being as she closed the door and pushed the bolt across.

* * *

It was midnight when the phone rang. Guessing it was Howard, Tiphanie stared morosely at it. She'd taken the bottle of brandy up to the studio with her, and had downed another small glass to try and numb her pain. It had only caused a deeper resentment

164

towards Howard to grow and fester inside her, though.

Before he'd turned up, some of the barriers between her and Kyle had begun to fall away; she'd felt as if a truly friendly rapport had been growing between them. Then Howard's little speech had made a mockery of all that, hadn't it? And now he'd got the cheek to phone her.

'I won't give you the satisfaction of speaking to me again,' she hissed at the phone.

But the insistent trill grated on her already raw nerves. Besides, it might wake Jack and Zoe, and she'd hate for them to see her sunk in this deep despair. She leapt out of the chair, stubbing her toe painfully in the process. Furiously, she grabbed the handset and poured forth her resentment.

'How you've got the temerity to take my best friend to bed and then state *you* forgive *me*, I'll never know. Did you really think I'd want anything to do with you after that? And why did you leave it almost a week before coming to find me? Did you think you'd give me time to mourn what Felicity had and I hadn't? You're pathetic and feeble, Howard, and I'd never go or want to go to bed with someone like you. I want a *real* man, a caring man, one I truly love — and not an apology for the male species.'

After replacing the handset, Tiphanie giggled and clapped her hands. 'I didn't know I possessed such eloquence! Perhaps it was those two small brandies. And Howard was obviously struck dumb. I'd have loved to see his face while he was listening.'

She immediately felt much better. It had done her good to get all that resentment out of her system. But fancy Howard being vain enough to think she'd still want him! She'd never realised how vain he was before.

Suddenly the idea for a new Frolic character based on Howard emerged. 'Vain-Brain Frolic,' she chortled. She always found it easy and satisfying to caricature somebody she was mad at or disliked. And, after fingering through some of the compilation CDs she'd made especially for working to, she decided to play the one containing the opening motif from Beethoven's *Fifth*: 'Fate Knocking at the Door'.

With the music playing softly in the background, she sat at her drawing board and doodled until she'd produced a satisfactory head and body shape. She resisted the temptation to turn the volume up when Carly Simon's 'You're So Vain' started to play, and instead reached for the lined paper she always used when creating a new character. The lines helped her keep everything in proportion.

First she concentrated on facial features, drawing Vain-Brain's face from every conceivable angle. Then the back of his head, his neck, and then his body. She drew him standing, sitting, running, leaning nonchalantly against a door, driving, eating, stretching, bending. Never forgetting that his main characteristic was vanity, Tiphanie brought Vain-Brain to life. Whatever he was doing, wherever he was, it always seemed as though he were preening.

She drew a thought bubble above his head with a picture of him holding up his hands and saying 'Woah!' as a crowd of women walked towards him, simpering. Oh, he thought he was God's gift to women, all right. 'I never realised just how much Howard thought of himself before.' She chuckled and looked across at Marmaduke curled on the edge of her desk. 'You never liked him, did you, Duke? You were quite right to feel the way you did about him.'

Marmaduke blinked as if agreeing, then yawned widely and went to sleep. Clever puss is right about that as well, Tiphanie thought. It's three-thirty; more than time I went to sleep, too. She stretched her weary limbs before making her way out of the studio and down to the bedroom.

★　★　★

In the cottage across the river, Kyle watched the lights in the smock mill go out. It had been him and not Howard on the receiving end of Tiphanie's tirade. He'd phoned to apologise for the taunts he'd thrown at her when leaving. He'd been aware she'd thought it was Howard the second she started talking on the phone, but there'd been no chance for him to tell her otherwise. Really, he should have hung up; but, immediately realising he'd misjudged her at Lanleigh, he'd carried on listening.

He hadn't entirely misjudged her, though, he thought grimly as, annoyed with himself for sitting thinking about her until now, he made his way to bed. There was still Tristan . . . and that character wrapped in a towel the other day. She was still a feckless flirt who couldn't or wouldn't make time for her true responsibilities. Scowling, he set his alarm clock. He had to catch a train to London in four hours; he'd wasted precious sleeping time thinking about Ms Tiphanie Timpson.

*　*　*

Tiphanie couldn't sleep, so she was glad when Crystal jumped up on the bed and settled down just below the pillow. Stroking the cat and hearing the soft purrs made her feel less lonely. She kept telling herself it was because she'd slept all day, or that working on her new character had made her overtired. In the end she admitted it was thoughts of Kyle keeping her awake.

Turning Howard into a cartoon character had purged him from her system, but it had also made room for Kyle to dominate her thoughts. So, sighing, Tiphanie allowed those thoughts entry. It might have been easier if she could have concentrated only on his cold, hard, angry side . . . but the gentle Kyle and the Kyle hurting from sad memories, the Kyle she longed to comfort and cherish, kept getting in the way. Perhaps the reason she'd experienced her mixed-up feelings for him from the start was because her soul had recognised the sadness in Kyle's.

'I wonder if it was a close relation — or maybe his girlfriend — who was killed in the motorbike accident,' she murmured to Crystal. If it *was* his girlfriend, that would explain a few things. Maybe Kyle felt guilty when he was attracted to someone; and that was why, earlier on in the kitchen, he'd pushed her away after kissing her. Because Tiphanie knew for sure he'd been aware of the undeniable magnetism that had been building between them.

Trying to thrust away the memory of how his body had felt against hers, she thumped the pillow, then apologised to Crystal for disturbing her. Maybe it was Kyle's wife who had been killed, and he can't live with the thought of anyone taking her place even temporarily. Maybe she had red hair and that's why he reacts the way he does to me. Maybe . . .

But, finally, overcome by emotions and exhaustion, she fell asleep. It was a fitful one, though, and every time she jerked awake, images of Kyle were running through her head.

★   ★   ★

Kyle had found it hard getting to sleep. In fact, when his alarm clock went off he felt as though he'd only just closed his eyes. He felt tired and bruised inside. Scarcely up to a creative discussion with his agent. He grimaced at his reflection as he shaved. How a woman like Tiphanie could get under his skin, he didn't know. He was as bad as all the other poor suckers. No, he wasn't. Not quite. He'd somehow managed to stop kissing her. It had been an effort, though. That kiss had been one for his tired soul to melt into.

And now was not the time to remember it; he had a train to catch.

Coincidentally, the first person Kyle saw after parking his car in the station car park was one of Tiphanie's men. The character who'd been wrapped in a towel was helping a pretty, and obviously pregnant, blonde out of Tristan's car.

As Kyle looked at him, with unsavoury thoughts running through his mind, the man looked up. 'Hello, didn't you call on Tiphanie the other day?' he asked. 'You spotted me in what must have seemed a compromising situation.' He turned to the woman at his side. 'Remember, Kay? I told you someone called at Tris's just after Tiphanie had dug some slivers of glass out of my back.'

'Just as you were making the grand gesture of going upstairs to get dressed,' Kay said, laughing. 'Poor Tiphanie. Anyone who didn't know her would have jumped to the wrong conclusions. Is she still staying at Tristan's?' she asked, looking at Kyle.

'She is.'

'I must call in and see her. I haven't seen her for ages; she leads such a hectic life. Dave said she's got the twins with her. They're adorable, and if I were their mother I'd want them with me all the time. I wouldn't put my career first. Still, I suppose it must be hard not to when you've got fans and followers to please, and it's nothing to do with me anyway.'

'My wife has developed strong views on motherhood recently.' Dave smiled and indicated Kay's bump. 'If you see Tiphanie, will you tell her we'll have our own car back on Monday, and I'll leave Tristan's in the long-stay car park? We'd better get a move on, darling,' he added, taking Kay's arm. 'We don't want to miss our train.'

'It was nice meeting you, Mr . . . Mr . . . ?' Kay said.

'Kyle Cooper,' he replied somewhat bemusedly. Then he realised he was also likely to miss his train if he didn't hurry, though he'd half a mind to text his agent to cancel the appointment and go back home. Or, rather, go over to Marsh View to speak to Tiphanie. He owed her a couple of apologies.

Then, shrugging, he loped off to the ticket office. He'd long since learned it wasn't a good idea to let his personal life interfere with his writing career. His agent had a proposition for him that sounded interesting. If he cancelled the appointment, someone else might benefit. Apologising to Tiphanie would have to wait.

Nevertheless, it was hard to put her out of his mind. He usually enjoyed partaking of breakfast on the early-morning train to London; today Tiphanie's image intruded, spoiling his appetite.

Bright red hair with a temper to match, he reminded himself. Smoky-grey eyes which could fill with anger and passion, with mischief and with hurt. He sighed aloud as he remembered the hurt in those eyes last night. He'd stormed off without giving her a chance to explain things. Though he had phoned to apologise and check if she was all right.

But she didn't know it was you, said his inner voice. She thought it was Howard and you didn't enlighten her, you just listened.

If I hadn't listened, I wouldn't be realising that I owed her an apology. Two apologies, he corrected himself, thinking of Dave. Then he scowled. There was still Tristan and the way she led her life. He didn't approve of it at all. No, Ms Tiphanie Timpson was definitely *not* the type of woman he wanted to get involved with.

Who are you kidding? That inner voice was at it again. Remember the way she responded when you kissed her? Remember how she felt in your arms? Remember, too, the sympathy that flowed from her when you told her about the crash and your height vertigo? The confidence in her voice when you confessed to being a wuss and she said: 'That's rubbish. You'd have climbed right to the top of the tree if I'd needed you to'?

Kyle was aware of his lips turning upwards with amusement. What a sight she'd made climbing down the tree, cat in arms and that silly shortie nightdress covering even less than it was designed to. She'd accused him of ogling just before she'd fainted. He had been as well. Her descent had been a delight to watch. And it all happened because of a barking dog and two ginger cats. He pushed his uneaten breakfast away, signalled for more coffee, and took out his notebook and a 'Paper Mate InkJoy' pen. He always preferred getting the first draft of a story or article down on paper rather than his laptop.

He spent the rest of his journey writing. He could write anywhere as long as there was no loud music distracting him. He'd developed his own peculiar shorthand; it wouldn't bother him if curious fellow travellers tried to see what he was writing, there was no way they'd make any sense of it.

His pen flew faster and faster over the pages. This was going to be one of the best humorous short stories he'd ever written, though he wouldn't submit it anywhere. He didn't stop thinking about Tiphanie as he wrote. She was very much in his mind.

7

Despite feeling and looking rather the worse for wear when she got up, Tiphanie was determined to go on the outing planned for yesterday. 'If you run up the tree this morning, you'll just have to stay there,' she told Crystal and Marmaduke as she shooed them out. 'Today, whatever happens, I'm going to Peterborough. A change of scenery and a chat with my editor will do me good.'

'And going to Wansford Station, too?' Zoe asked, coming up behind her. 'Will that do you good? At least talking to trains will be better than talking to yourself.'

'I was talking to Crystal and Duke,' Tiphanie replied. 'But, yes, we'll go to the station after I've had a chat with my editor. But before either of those things, we'll have to do some food shopping. There's a good choice of shops and a great Oriental supermarket.

'And I may be a while at the magazine publishers. I worked on a new Frolic character last night, or rather, the early hours of this morning. I want to discuss him with Natasha.'

'Working half the night is why you've got purple bags under your eyes,' said Jack. 'I was worried in case it was the fall you had that was making you look so yuck. You can leave Zoe and me in that bookshop in the arcade while you're with the magazine peeps,' he continued, giving Tiphanie no time to comment on his previous remarks. 'The manager will keep an eye on us, he knows us from when Tristan does his book signings. We can look for that book Kyle told us about, Zo.'

'It's one by Paul Gallico,' Zoe told Tiphanie. '*The Snow Goose*. Kyle said a lighthouse not that far from here was used in the story. And the pictures of the lighthouse remind him of this place. Did Kyle tell you he used to live here? I wonder why he moved to his little cottage across the river. Marsh View is heaps more exciting.'

Tiphanie fought down the urge to ask the twins if Kyle had mentioned a wife or girlfriend living here with him. She didn't want to start thinking about him and his attitude towards her again; she wanted to get back to a comparatively uncomplicated way of life. Though right now, she thought, Zoe sounded rather bunged up.

'Do you feel OK, Zoe?' she asked. 'You haven't got a cold, have you?' She felt Zoe's forehead but it was cool enough.

'Just a bit sniffly,' Zoe replied. 'I think it was the soap I used when I got washed. It's got quite a strong flowery smell.'

'She often gets the sniffles after she's washed her face,' Jack said. 'That's why she doesn't wash it too often,' he said, grinning.

'At least I wash behind my ears,' said Zoe. 'You hardly ever — '

'That's enough, you two. You haven't

got time to wind each other up.' Though at least them getting at each other had taken their minds off Kyle.

'Remind me to call in at the jeweller's before I go to see Natasha,' she said. 'I left my ring there to be altered.'

'Your mum's wedding band?' queried Zoe. 'I'd noticed you weren't wearing it. I didn't ask why in case you'd lost it.'

'I almost did,' confessed Tiphanie. 'It happened the last time I was in Peterborough. It slipped off my finger. Luckily, I heard the little clink when it fell. I took it straight into the nearest jeweller's to get it made a bit smaller.'

'Do you still put it on your wedding ring finger when you go to the magazine publishers?' Jack asked. 'Remember when we came to the offices with you and we had to pretend to be your children?'

Tiphanie laughed. 'Yes, I still let the managing editor think I'm married and you two are mine. It's because he's got this thing about wanting to use only married freelancers. He thinks anyone who's single might spend too much time living it up and be too tired to meet a deadline. Of course, Natasha and the other editors know the truth,' she added virtuously. 'And I never actually said I was married . . . I just let him jump to his own conclusions.'

'He couldn't help jumping to them what with you wearing Grandma's wedding ring and us calling you Mum,' Zoe said, giggling. 'I didn't lie, either, when he asked what I thought of my mother's work. I told him I thought my mother was very clever.'

★　★　★

Tiphanie's meeting with Natasha went well. But she added further to her subterfuge when Angus Gilbert, the managing editor, asked how the twins were. 'They're fine,' she told him, twisting her mother's wedding band that now fit snugly on her own wedding ring finger. 'I've left them in the bookshop, and when I leave here we're going to see the trains at Wansford Station. They go back to school on Monday so I'll be able to get more work done.'

'That's good,' he rumbled. 'I take it Natasha has told you about our new magazine?'

'The 'Story Magazine'. Yes, she has. I'm looking forward to illustrating the stories. I'll make a start next week. I've got a set of proofs for most of them here, and Natasha is going to email me copies of the rest as soon as she gets them.'

'Don't get carried away with the artwork. We only want one illustration for each story. That's why we thought of you. You've got a knack for showing a lot in one simple picture.'

'I'll let you have roughs of everything first,' promised Tiphanie. 'Have you got a flat-plan yet? I'd like to see where the advertising pages fall.'

'There's a copy of the flat-plan and of the adverts in there.' Natasha pointed to a large folder. 'We worked hard on getting the right adverts. As you'll see, they're mostly complementary to the stories. And there are a couple of ads there that would be good for your *Fenland Frolics* special. The one for men's cologne would be ideal to follow a story you've used your new character in. I think Vain-Brain Frolic will prove to be a very popular addition,' she added with a smile.

'If Tiphanie were footloose and fancy-free, she'd be too busy thinking about her latest boyfriend or nightclubbing to produce all the work we want from her.'

Tiphanie hid a smile. She was often tempted to produce a caricature of the managing editor. He never lost an opportunity to point out how right his views were.

But his words did make her resolve once again to stop thinking about Kyle. And, after discussing a few more points with Natasha, she hurried away to collect the twins.

When Tiphanie entered the book-shop, she saw that Jack and Zoe were with Tad. 'What are you doing here?' she asked. 'Is Linda with you?'

'No, she's taken our German guests to London for the day. I'm meeting them off the four o'clock train. I didn't go with them because I had an appointment at the Planning Office. How about you lot coming for a celebration lunch? My latest plans for a barn conversion have been approved.'

'That's certainly worth celebrating,' Tiphanie said, pleased for her twin. 'I've got something to celebrate, too. Not quite as big league as yours, but it's another string to my bow.' She looked down at Jack and Zoe. 'It's up to you two to make the choice. Celebrating with Tad, or going to see the trains?'

'Celebrating,' they replied without hesitation. 'It's great at the station, but we're going there on a day trip with the school in June, so not going today won't matter. And we could go with Tad to meet Linda off the London train, and see the German visitors as well.'

'Plus,' Zoe added, 'we don't often get to eat lunch with Tad in a posh hotel.'

'Who said anything about a posh hotel? I was thinking of going to a chippie or a burger bar,' teased their uncle. 'I've already spent a fortune this morning. A set of books for Linda's birthday, which is why I came here in the first place, and I also bought a rather nice copy of *The Snow Goose* for the two pests,' he informed Tiphanie, answering her querying look. 'Their new hero told them about it, apparently. He sounds quite an interesting chap. Rescued you from a fierce dog, I understand. Even though you'd previously burst a cushion all over him.'

'Kyle Cooper isn't worth talking about. He's self-opinionated, bad-tempered, and doesn't give a person a chance to explain anything. He . . . he . . . Oh, I don't know.' He would have overcome his fear to help me down the tree, though; his hands were gentle and caring when I fell, he put me to bed and watched the twins while I slept all day, he's haunted by unhappy memories and I wanted to love him better, he despises me and thinks I'm a tramp, she listed silently. 'He doesn't even like cats. That's the sort of person he is,' she told Tad.

'Did you have a row with him last night after Zo and I went to bed?' asked Jack with interest.

'It's a waste of breath discussing him,' Tiphanie replied.

'I think the lady doth protest too much,' Tad said, grinning.

'But maybe we shouldn't have bought this CD for her, Zo,' Jack said in a whisper clearly meant for Tiphanie to hear. 'I mean, she does like The Corrs, but maybe one song on the disc . . . '

'You mean 'Toss the Feathers'.' Zoe giggled.

'It's sure to remind her of the burst cushion episode,' Tad agreed.

'Oh, gang up on me, why don't you?' said Tiphanie. 'I'm not staying to listen to any more rubbish. I'll go and do something worth doing like finding the manager to thank him for keeping an eye on Jack and Zoe.'

When Tiphanie returned, Jack pointed to the CD. 'There's a good connection here, Tiphanie,' he said. 'Look, one of the songs is called 'Runaway', and that's what you did just then. You ran away.'

'Well, connect hunger to food and food to hotel,' she said. 'I'm starving. It must be all the exciting news. Lead the way, Tad.'

During their meal — in a restaurant more than posh enough to delight Jack and Zoe — Tad said casually, 'I'm planning to move back in with you and Dad for a while, Tiphanie. Linda's been offered a three-month contract in Germany as a costume supervisor and designer for a television drama. I think that's more or less the same as a wardrobe mistress.'

'I'm really pleased for Linda,' Tiphanie said. And she was. But she also guessed why Tad wanted to come and stay in the family home while his wife was away. Aware of her colour rising, she said, 'But I don't see why you should expect me to look after *your* clothes and feed you while she's away.'

'Don't spoil things by getting all het up, Tiph, we'll discuss it later,' said Tad.

'Right, we'll talk about it at the station while we're waiting for Linda,' Tiphanie replied.

Following Tad in her car, Tiphanie told the twins she wanted time alone with Tad when they got to the station.

'Are you going to get really cross with him?' Zoe asked.

'I'm just going to let him know I am not his doormat,' Tiphanie said. 'He and Tristan try to take advantage of me too often.'

'You mean, like Tristan going off and leaving you on your own to look after us?' Jack asked.

'Mmm, but I didn't really mind that. I like having you around.' Tiphanie didn't want her niece and nephew to think she felt they'd been forced onto her.

'Except I don't want you around for the next few minutes,' she added a short time later when she'd parked the car in the station car park. 'Just you wait by the car while I go and talk to that brother of mine.'

★   ★   ★

Kyle, walking towards where he'd parked his car that morning, couldn't miss seeing Tiphanie — bending slightly as she talked to someone who was in a car he didn't recognise. Though actually, from her stance, it looked more as if she was angry and arguing with the occupant.

A couple of minutes later, he saw the twins standing by Tiphanie's car on the opposite side of the car park. He would have carried on to his own vehicle, but they'd obviously seen him because they called to him. They looked excited, and he couldn't bring himself just to wave and carry on, so he walked over to them. Besides, if he were honest, he wanted to know why Tiphanie was angry.

'What's wrong with her now?' he asked gesturing towards Tiphanie. 'It looks as if she's berating the man in that car.'

'Tad wants to move back in with her but she doesn't want him to,' said Zoe. 'She said she doesn't see why she should look after his clothes and feed him while — '

'Never mind all that, Zo,' said Jack. 'We want to show Kyle our book, don't we?'

'Oh, yes. We met Tad in the bookshop, and when he saw us looking at *The Snow Goose*, he bought it for us. And after that he took us and Tiphanie to a posh restaurant for lunch.'

Zoe began to list the food they'd had, and although he was in a hurry, Kyle listened — enjoying the little girl's descriptions.

'Then Tiphanie started to get cross because she didn't want to be treated like a doormat.' Zoe giggled. 'That's a funny saying, isn't it? But, anyway, she saved getting cross until we got here. And — '

'Shut up, Zo,' said Jack, nudging her before he looked at Kyle. 'Look, Kyle, aren't these pictures great?' He carefully turned the pages of the book.

'It's a very nice edition,' Kyle said. 'I'll have to go now, though. I want to get to the post office before it closes. That's one problem about living off the beaten track. We have to collect our own mail.'

'Can we come over to yours to say goodbye to you before we go back to Grandma's?' asked Zoe. 'We're going on Sunday. Tiphanie's staying longer. I wish we could stay with her, but it's easier for us to get to school from Grandma's.'

Zoe hadn't sounded annoyed or resentful, just matter-of-fact, and she and Jack certainly seemed happy and carefree. Nevertheless, Kyle couldn't get his head around the way Tiphanie was bringing them up.

He glanced across the car park and noticed another woman had joined Tiphanie — and Tiphanie had an indignant look on her face as she was talking to her. Against his will, he couldn't help thinking how appealing Tiphanie looked, even when she was annoyed.

'Can we, Kyle? Can we come and say goodbye?' Zoe asked again, breaking into his thoughts.

'Yes, come and see me,' Kyle replied, ruffling her hair. 'Bring the book with you and I'll have a better look at it.'

★　★　★

There were quite a few cars streaming out of the car park now, and to avoid feeling like a jaywalker, Tiphanie chose to walk around the perimeter to get back to her vehicle and collect the twins to take them to the station café, where

Linda had left her guests while coming to see if Tad had arrived.

She walked with a springy bounce to her step. She'd won the battle with Tad, thanks to Linda arriving at his parked car in time to hear the argument, and agreeing wholeheartedly that Tad should look after himself while she was away.

Tad had taken it well enough. He'd even seemed apologetic about having wanted her to run round after him. Tiphanie was glad about that: even though she knew she'd been in the right, she didn't like being at odds with her twin. She didn't like being at odds with anyone, really, and because Zoe and Jack had known she was about to argue with Tad, she decided she'd act the fool and creep up behind the car making silly noises.

She changed her mind, though, and decided to listen in, unseen, when she heard Zoe say to Jack, 'I can't understand why Tiphanie got so mad when Tad mentioned Kyle in the bookshop. Kyle's so handsome and so romantic.'

'Don't be so girly,' Jack scoffed. 'He's a jolly interesting person, that's all. I'm glad we saw him here and he said we could go over to his before we go back to Grandma's. I hope he shows us some of his cowboy stories. Remember, Zo, he told us about them yesterday. I think I'll write cowboy books when I become an author.'

'I thought you wanted to write science fiction like those books set on the marshes.'

'Well, maybe, but they aren't real sci-fi, you know. They're sort of spoof stories. That's why the heroes are called Marshians — spelt with 's' and 'h' instead of a 't'. I bet Kyle could write stories like those, he's quite funny sometimes.'

Tiphanie had second thoughts about acting the fool now. Her nephew and niece were so busy hero-worshipping Kyle-flipping-Cooper they probably wouldn't find anything she did was amusing.

So she stepped round the car to reach them and explained why she'd come the long way round. 'And Tad, Linda and their guests are waiting for us to join them in the café. The cars have driven off now so we'll walk across the car park to get there. We'll just stop for a quick drink, though. The cats have been on their own for ages.'

Tiphanie sat down next to her sister-in-law, and Jack and Zoe sat opposite her with Tad and the house-guests. They made a cheerful group as they chatted and drank coffee; or, in the twins' case, hot chocolate. And Jack and Zoe, always delighted to have an audience, showed the German family their new book with its pictures of a lighthouse.

'Tad bought it for us,' Zoe said, leaning across her brother to smile at him. 'Didn't you, Tad?'

'Tiphanie,' Linda said very quietly, holding a paper serviette to her mouth as if she was wiping it, 'Zoe called him Dad both times then. She hasn't done it for years, but she used to for a while after Anthony's death.'

'It's OK. It just sounded like she did because she's a bit sniffly. She blamed the soap for it earlier on, but I've noticed it a few times this week. I've a feeling she's getting a cold.'

Tiphanie glanced across at Zoe to see if she looked unwell. She didn't, though. Both she and Jack seemed to be in deep conversation with Tad and Linda's house guests.

'You'll have to visit Germany,' Herr Meier was telling them. 'We have a lot of interesting lighthouses. The Campen in Lower Saxony near the Ems estuary is our tallest lighthouse, and is also one of the tallest of its kind in the world.'

'You would like the Pilsum light-house,' said his wife. 'It is red and yellow and looks like a . . . a . . . ' She shrugged. 'A *spiralförmige Rutsch-bahn*.'

'A helter-skelter,' Linda translated from her side of the table.

'Cool,' said Jack. 'I mean nice,

interesting. This one in the book is quite near our other uncle's where we're staying. Tristan lives in a converted smock mill and it looks a bit like this lighthouse.'

'There are stone ledges circling it about half a metre below all the windows,' said Zoe. 'Tiphanie's cat, Marmaduke, jumped from a tree onto the ledge below the room Tristan uses as a studio.' Zoe went on to tell the tale of how they'd played music to try and coax him in through an open window.

Tiphanie laughed along with everyone else, hoping neither Jack nor Zoe would mention Kyle. But of course they did, in great detail.

'I think you've got an admirer, Tiphanie,' Linda whispered. Tiphanie, her mind annoyingly focused very much on thoughts and memories of Kyle, thought that was who Linda was referring to. Until Linda continued, 'Not your type, I don't think. Blue eyes, a crew cut, and wearing a rather loud tee-shirt.'

'That, I can do without,' Tiphanie told her. 'I'm off all men at the moment.'

'Even the twins' hero?' Linda laughed. 'He's rather dishy according to Zoe.'

'*Especially* the twins' hero,' Tiphanie retorted, and she got to her feet to make her farewells. 'Sorry to break things up, but we must get back for the cats. If Tristan's cat therapist knew we'd left Crystal for so long . . . ' She drew her finger across her throat and laughed before hustling Jack and Zoe away.

⋆ ⋆ ⋆

Tiphanie had been driving for about twenty minutes when she sighed as yet another set of traffic lights turned against her. She glanced uneasily in her mirror. Was she being paranoid or was the car behind following her? The driver was her 'admirer' from the café, of that she was sure — blue eyes, crew cut, and a loud tee-shirt.

Biting hard on her lip, she checked

for the third time that her car doors were locked, and decided to give a late signal and make a right turn when the lights changed. And if he followed behind her, she'd pull in somewhere and use her mobile to phone the police.

However, to her great relief, the car went straight on. 'Stupid woman,' she muttered.

'Who is?' Jack asked from the back seat.

'I am. I took a wrong turning. I was thinking about my work,' she fibbed. There was no point in letting the twins know she'd been worried and frightened. The episode had shaken her; it brought home just how vulnerable she still felt when driving without another adult in the car.

When they arrived at Marsh View, Zoe commented on Tiphanie's pallor.

'It's probably because I stayed up half the night working on my new character. I'll go to bed early tonight to make up for it. Look at the cats,' she said, glad to have a genuine reason for changing the subject. 'They're both sulking.'

'They haven't eaten, either,' Jack called from the kitchen. 'Shall I throw this away and put some new food down, Tiphanie?'

'I'll put them out first. They'll be more likely to eat after they've had a stroll around in the fresh air.'

'Can we go and play in the tree-house for a while?' Jack asked. 'We'll have a little while before it starts going dark.'

'It'll give you a chance to look at the stuff Natasha gave you,' Zoe added, pointing to the manila folder.

Tiphanie nodded, but knew she didn't feel like looking at flat-plans or proofs of the stories for the new magazine yet. Once she'd put the shopping away, she'd have a shower and get changed. She felt both hot and sticky, and cold and clammy.

It really was about time she stopped imagining she'd be a victim of a car attack. After all, it hadn't *actually* happened, had it? But that foggy night always came back to haunt her when other things were upsetting her. Things like that dog yesterday, and Howard turning up, and Kyle . . . 'No,' she said aloud. 'I will *not* think about him.'

★   ★   ★

Tiphanie felt better for her shower and was in her bedroom drying her hair when Zoe burst in. 'The cats went across the bridge,' she said. 'We couldn't stop them, we were in the tree-house. They're both in Kyle's garden now. Shall Jack and I go and fetch them?'

'I'd better come with you. Marmaduke is quite likely to run off. It's his way of protesting at being left inside. I've got to stay till Tris comes back, but if he's going to be away much longer, I'll get a cat-flap for the front door.'

Tiphanie pulled a tee-shirt on over her still-wet hair, and followed Zoe down the stairs and out of the front door.

As they hurried across the bridge, Zoe started singing the song from *Three Billy Goats Gruff*.

'Let's hope the big, bad troll, *fol-dee-rol*, doesn't threaten to eat us for his supper,' said Tiphanie. She had a feeling Kyle wasn't going to be any too pleased to see them. She knew he was home; his car was parked on the cottage driveway. Though of course, she thought hopefully, he might have gone for a run.

'They're both sitting in the rock garden,' Jack called. He'd run ahead and was peering over the gate. 'I expect there's some plants of that mint stuff cats like. Shall I go and knock on the door and ask Kyle if we can go and fetch them?' he added as Tiphanie and Zoe drew level with him.

'I'll go,' Tiphanie said. The rockery was beautiful and the whole garden a riot of spring flowers. It was obviously well-cared-for — though not in a regimented way. She couldn't blame Kyle for not wanting cats in it.

Opening the gate, she marched up the path with a confidence she was far from feeling. Part of her didn't want to approach Kyle, but if she'd let Jack be the one to do it, Kyle was likely to think she was afraid to face him. And, deep inside, was the knowledge that she wanted to see him, speak to him, and to hear his voice — even if it was full of sarcasm and derision.

I'm becoming addicted to him, she panicked. I keep telling myself to put him out of my mind, to stop thinking about him. But I can't keep him out of my heart, can't help imagining what it would be like to . . . She felt a warm blush spread over her cheeks and for a moment she wavered. Maybe she should let Jack be the one to knock at the door.

The decision was taken out of her hands. The door flew open and Kyle was standing there. His tall frame reached the top of the doorway, and there was anger in every line of his taut body as he glared down at her.

8

The allure of her damp hair straggling round her face and shoulders in frizzy orange streamers, her smallness with its false air of fragility, the quickly masked indecision in her smoky-grey eyes, her turned-up nose, her little chin jutting determinedly upwards, all served to fan his anger to a greater height. He would *not* allow her to get under his skin.

'I hope you've come to remove those animals,' he grated, pointing towards the cats.

★ ★ ★

His minatory tone titillated her nerve ends. Aware of a coiling sensation deep inside, Tiphanie wondered dismally if she was turned on by anger. Her lips were dry; she licked them and then looked over towards the cats to avoid

207

looking at Kyle.

His hand snaked out and he put his fingers under her chin, turning her to face him again. 'I warned Tristan when he moved in that I didn't want his cat using my garden to — ' He broke off and then drew his mouth into a thin line.

Probably unwilling to swear in front of Jack and Zoe, thought Tiphanie — who, she registered, were standing one on either side of her and eyeing Kyle with interest. She put an arm around both of them and manoeuvred them along with herself to one side as Kyle stepped onto the path.

His dark green cords fitted snugly to his thighs, his hips and his waist. Tiphanie gazed in enthrallment at the rise and fall of his chest under the cream crew-necked sweater — she could see the dark shadow of his body hair through the lightweight material. She breathed in deeply, and the tang of his aftershave or cologne permeated her nostrils, mingling with the salty aroma carried on the light breeze from the nearby saltings.

He'd placed his hands on his hips, thumbs hooked through his belt, sleeves pushed back as usual, showing the tenseness of the muscles in his forearms. Suddenly, all her fascination with him evaporated, and now the aggression emanating from him annoyed her. Before she could say anything, he spoke.

Just the one word: 'Well?'

Tiphanie wondered how just one word could hold so much contempt and cause the hairs on the back of her neck to rise.

She was vaguely aware of Jack and Zoe walking towards the rockery. They'd probably sensed Kyle's anger and thought it best to move away. 'Well, what?' She attempted to glare up at him but a gust of breeze blew her hair over her eyes and spoilt the effect. Frustrated, she thrust her hair back and could feel Kyle's eyes on her. Then his index finger tapped her ring.

'I see you wore your wedding ring for today's meeting.'

It was the last thing she'd expected to hear. Her hand froze and she was sure her bewilderment must be showing on her face. And she was struggling to control the fluttering sensations his second light touch in less than five minutes had evoked.

'It wouldn't do to let him think I was single and had time and money to gad around,' she replied, quickly transferring the ring to its more usual place on her right hand and trying not to think how Kyle had touched the ring seconds before. 'I have to keep my payments coming in. I don't like pretending I'm — '

'Of all the deceitful things to do,' he interrupted harshly. 'You must be making a reasonable living, but that's not enough for you, is it? You have to make that poor sucker keep paying out even when you're living with — '

'I don't know what you're talking about, Kyle. I wear the ring on my wedding finger when — '

Kyle continued as though she hadn't spoken. 'I thought my wife was bad enough, but she's an angel compared to you.'

So it wasn't his wife who was killed in the motorbike crash, was Tiphanie's first thought. Then it was speedily followed by an anguished realisation . . . He's married.

Kyle's next words halted her thoughts. 'You're beneath all contempt. 'Well, what?' you asked me a few seconds ago. Well, get your cats, and then get out of my sight — and stay out of it. I never want to have the misfortune of seeing you again.'

'We've got them, Tiphanie. Both of them,' said Jack.

'Mum . . . Crystal scratched him, but it's not bleeding,' Zoe added.

The twins' voices broke through the hurt and torment Kyle's words had caused, though for a second she had to grind her knuckles into her eyes to hold back the threatened tears. Even though her vision was misty, it was clear enough to see the look of contempt Kyle cast upon her. She couldn't understand why he was so disgusted, so angry. She wasn't harming anyone by letting the managing editor think she was married. And why should Kyle think the managing editor was a sucker for paying her? She earned her money, for heaven's sake.

Tiphanie opened her mouth to ask him, but couldn't get any words past the lump in her throat. She turned slowly away, every movement an effort, and walked down the path and out of the gate, leaving Jack and Zoe to follow her. She heard Kyle's voice, softer now, as he spoke to the twins. But she didn't look back. She couldn't bear to.

★　★　★

The evening passed in a blur of pain and hurt. When Jack and Zoe had eaten and gone to bed, she relived that scene with Kyle over and over again. She still couldn't understand why he thought the managing editor was a sucker. And what right had Kyle to condemn her for her harmless pretence?

After all, even though *he* really was married, Kyle had kissed her; and for a glorious nanosecond had held her like a lover. OK, so he had been the one to end it, to push her away. But after he'd banged her back, he'd been so apologetic, and she'd seen the kind, gentle, and caring side of him that she'd perceived a couple of times before. She wondered which Kyle his wife knew best — the loving one, or the sarcastic, macho, alpha male.

Thinking about it, surely it was likely Kyle and his wife were separated? If not, why had there been no sign of her? And would Kyle have spent the whole day and most of the evening here yesterday looking after Jack and Zoe while she slept after the fright she'd had? Though, of course, she might be away on holiday or for work.

But she didn't really care where Kyle's wife was, or if they were separated.

Yes, you do, argued her inner voice. No matter what he's said, what he thinks of you, even though he would be so wrong for you with all his different moods and sides, you still feel for him what you've never felt for any other man.

Not true, she argued back. What I feel for him is dislike.

* * *

Tiphanie dreamt that night. She dreamt she was walking across the bridge, but when she got to the middle of it she plunged down, down into the river below. As she splashed and struggled in the water, she heard Kyle's voice: 'You're beneath all contempt, Tiphanie. Put your ring on your wedding finger and force that poor sucker to pull you out.'

Then came the managing editor's

voice. 'I only employ married freelancers. You tricked me, Tiphanie. You're fired.'

She saw Kyle kissing an angel who'd appeared next to him on the river bank, and she knew it was his wife. Then a huge, hairy Alsatian dog jumped into the water and, barking, began chasing her. There was a tree growing in the river, but every time she tried to climb it, it moved out of reach. And the Alsatian was close to her now, showing its huge teeth, and she couldn't put a great enough distance between them.

'Help me, Kyle. Please help me.'

Kyle laughed. A mocking laugh that filled her dream. 'You're beneath contempt and I never want to have the misfortune of seeing you again.'

The Alsatian was gaining on her, then its mouth closed around her arm. Tiphanie screamed and the scream woke her. But the dog was still there, a huge menacing shadow looming over her.

Her light went on and Jack and Zoe

dashed into her bedroom. 'Tiphanie. What's wrong?'

Half-laughing, half-crying, Tiphanie pointed to Marmaduke. 'I had a nightmare about that Alsatian. When I woke up, Duke was on the bed standing over me and I thought he was the dog.'

'You should have stayed asleep longer,' Zoe said. 'Kyle might have wandered into your dream and rescued you.'

'Oh, he was in my dream all right,' she muttered under her breath. 'But he was far off rescuing me.' Somehow, she managed to pull herself together, and was glad her voice sounded reasonably normal when she suggested that they all went down to the kitchen and she'd make some pancakes.

'Pancakes,' exclaimed Jack.

'Duke likes that idea as well.' Zoe giggled and pointed to the cat who'd jumped down from the bed and was standing alert, tail upright and facing the door.

'What a shame you don't have more

nightmares, Tiphanie,' Jack said. 'Oh, I don't mean I want you to feel scared, but you've never offered to make us pancakes in the middle of the night before.'

There are a lot of 'never before's in my life right now, gloomed Tiphanie as she got out of bed and put her dressing gown on. Never before have I met such a complicated, complex person as Kyle. Never before have my heart, my body, reacted to someone the way they do to him; and never before have I swung between attraction and dislike and despair for someone.

But it's got to stop. I don't ever want the misfortune of seeing him again, either. How dare he kiss me the way he did when he's got a wife somewhere? A wife who's an angel compared to me. If they *are* separated, I bet he drove her away with his mocking sarcasm.

'You haven't changed your mind about making pancakes, have you, Tiphanie?' Zoe asked anxiously.

Tiphanie forced a smile. 'Of course

not. I said we'd have them and we will. Go and put your dressing gowns on before you come down.'

* * *

It was four o'clock in the morning, and what with the fun of making and eating the pancakes, Jack and Zoe were now almost asleep again. Yawning and laughing, they went back up to bed. Tiphanie knew it was pointless for her to do that. She wouldn't be able to sleep; her nightmare was still too recent.

She was still upset by it, and the earlier incident when she'd thought that man in the car might be following her was playing on her mind as well. It disturbed her because she really ought to be over that fear — the panic attacks, or whatever name a doctor might give them, by now.

'Wimp, drama queen, paranoid, neurotic,' she told herself as she tidied the kitchen. But acknowledging that didn't bring back her serenity. She decided to go up to the studio and read through the material Natasha had given her for the Story Magazine.

Tiphanie's panacea for all ills was often her work or a good read. And now, as dawn was breaking over the salt marshes, the stories Natasha had given her to read were certainly pushing her troubled thoughts right to the back of her mind. They were brilliant, mainly humorous, verging on the ridiculous.

'Slapstick comedy,' she said, chuckling to herself. 'The magazine should do well. Everybody needs laughter in their lives.'

She got up to select a CD to play, and reached for her pad and pencil to rough out some ideas. She'd be able to make good use of speech bubbles and captions to emphasise the zanier aspect of each story. A hilarious one about waxworks — based, Tiphanie felt sure, on Dickens' Mrs Jarley — caused tears of laughter to flow, and she had to sit back and take a rest from her sketching.

When she'd recovered, her glance fell on a couple of lines written in pencil at the end of the story. 'Not an instruction for the typesetter,' she observed, spotting her own name.

It was, in fact, a brief message from Natasha, her editor, instructing her to take a good look at the advertisement which would follow the waxwork story. Curiously, Tiphanie riffled through the photocopied pages in a separate folder marked 'ADS'. She had no trouble in spotting the one Natasha meant.

'What a fantastic idea,' Tiphanie murmured, sending silent thanks to Natasha for drawing her attention to it. 'I'd have studied all the ads anyway,' she said to Marmaduke, who'd strolled in and jumped up onto the desk. 'But probably not until a later date.'

Seeing this particular one now, after a certain old fear had so recently come back to haunt her, was an act of providence. Too impatient to go down and fetch her laptop from her bedroom to shop online, she wrote out an order, giving her home address in Lynn. She presumed she'd be back there in ten days, the waiting time for delivery — though she hadn't yet heard from Tristan regarding his return — and reached for an envelope to put it in.

Then she gasped in delight as the address of the suppliers registered. They were only about twelve miles away. Seeing as Jack and Zoe wouldn't be here, she'd go there on Monday. It would be better to collect it than having it delivered, anyway. If Madge was at the house, cleaning up after the decorators, she'd have a fit if she were the one to accept it. Tiphanie laughed as she imagined that scene.

'What's so funny?' asked Zoe, coming into the studio. 'What time did you get up, Tiphanie? It's only seven o'clock now.'

'I didn't bother going back to bed. And this . . . ' Tiphanie reached for the advertisement to show it to her niece and explained the reason for her mirth. 'But Madge won't have to take delivery because I've decided to go and collect one instead. It'll be fun choosing my own.'

'It will,' agreed Zoe. 'I won't tell Jack about it. You can fool him with it one day. It's a shame you've got to take us home tomorrow. Are you coming back here after that?'

'I'll have to. I don't know when Tristan's going to phone to let me know how long he'll be away.'

'Lucky you, staying on.' Zoe sighed dramatically. 'You'll be able to see Kyle every day. Look, there he is now, going for a jog. You could go with him, Tiphanie. Jack and I will be all right on our own for a while.'

Tiphanie tried really hard not to get up and have a look. But she couldn't resist the chance of catching a glimpse of Kyle. So much for putting him out of my mind, she berated herself as she joined Zoe at the window and stared yearningly across the river.

Was it her imagination, or did he glance across at Marsh View? If so, he was probably wishing she wasn't here. Tiphanie turned away, annoyed at herself for having given into the temptation of looking at Kyle.

'How about we do some cooking and baking after breakfast?' she said to Zoe. 'We can concoct something delicious with the food we got from the Oriental supermarket.'

'Picnicky food would be good,' Zoe said. 'Then Jack and I can have a feast up in the tree-house. A sort of farewell-for-now feast because we're going home tomorrow.'

★　★　★

Three hours later, Tiphanie tied a rope to the handle of a basket full of food and drink. 'Climb up to the tree-house, taking the other end of the rope with you, and then you can haul the basket up,' she said to Jack and Zoe as they walked over to the tree.

They'd just accomplished this successfully when Tiphanie heard the phone ringing over the twins' cheers. 'Enjoy your feast,' she called as she hurried away, hoping whoever was phoning wouldn't hang up before she got inside.

'You sound a bit breathless, Tizz,' the caller said after she'd managed to grab the phone before it stopped ringing. 'Is Crystal all right? No problems, I hope?'

'Tristan. About time, too,' Tiphanie said. 'I was outside with the twins,' she added.

'That's another reason I phoned. I wanted to get back before they went — '

'You've still time to do that. They aren't going till tomorrow. Right now they're having a picnic in the tree-house — a farewell feast before they go, Zoe called it.'

'What tree-house? Never mind, tell me later. The thing is, Tizz, I've still a lot to do. Are you OK to stay on another week?'

'I suppose so. I can work as well here as anywhere.' *Unless thoughts of Kyle distract me*, she added silently.

'Seen anything of Kyle?' Tristan asked as though he'd read her mind.

'Actually, it was him who built the tree-house.'

'Ah, so you've got friendly, have you?'

'Hardly. I've had a couple of run-ins with him. He can be so arrogant, to say the least. I didn't realise he was married. I haven't seen his wife though. What's she like? Have you met her?'

'She's an absolute horror. Plays at being helpless and needy, and makes out she just wants someone to love and care for and the same in return. In reality, she's as hard as nails. I took her out once — I didn't know Kyle at the time, but when I told her I was a writer, she said her ex-husband was too.'

Tiphanie couldn't stop the feelings of relief and delight coiling through her body at the words 'ex-husband'. But Tristan was still talking and she listened eagerly.

'Apparently, Kyle became quite successful soon after they'd separated.

America and Spain suddenly couldn't get enough of his Westerns. Full-length books, pocket books, short stories — you name it, they wanted it. Anyway, even though she was a big earner herself, Denise felt he should give her more maintenance.

'She spent most of the evening bitching about Kyle and trying to work out how successful I was. Luckily, she didn't consider me successful enough. I never saw her again. Not to speak to. Her picture was in one of the Sunday colour supplements a few weeks ago. She'd just become engaged to a property millionaire old enough to be her grandfather.'

'That explains his bitterness towards women,' said Tiphanie. 'It must have hurt his pride when she got engaged to an old man.'

'I don't know about that. He was probably glad to be shot of her. Mind you, she's a beauty to look at. Long blonde hair and a face like an angel's. I caught sight of her visiting him once or twice before her engagement had been announced. I knew she was bad news, but I had to remind myself of that, and guessed she'd probably visited Kyle to give him a bad time.'

'He probably deserved it,' Tiphanie said, knowing she was being unfair.

'Fallen for him, have you?' Tristan taunted. 'He'd suit you actually, Tizz. You always did need a strong hand.'

An image of Kyle's hand running down her face crossed her mind and, annoyed, she said, 'I'd have to be pretty desperate to fall for someone like him. I'd better go and check on the twins now, Tris. Come back as soon as you can.' With that, she hung up quickly before Tristan could realise just *how* desperate she was for Kyle to feel love and not dislike for her.

She wandered to the front door and stood on the top step. To check on Jack and Zoe, she told herself. So why, then, was she looking over at Kyle's cottage and not towards the tree?

Even though he was free to love her,

to be physically attracted to her, it didn't make any difference. He let his contempt for her overrule any other feeling. There was no use in pretending there could be a happy ending. He thought she took love where she could find it. He was the only one she wanted to love her, the only one she wanted to love. He possessed her heart and her soul. She wanted him to possess . . .

The blood pounded in her veins, her need for him startling her as it coiled through her body until even her toes felt as though they were on fire. Though maybe that's because Marmaduke and Crystal are sitting on my feet, she thought, trying for a touch of humour to rid herself of other thoughts.

'I've got to do something to take my mind off him,' she said, looking down at the cats. 'I can't stand here like a wanton. I'll take the twins to the swimming baths; they'll have digested their food enough by the time we get there. And I will swim myself back into sensibility.'

9

'Tiphanie, we've packed our travel bags and tidied our room, so is it OK if we go and say goodbye to Kyle? He did say we could,' Zoe added, and Tiphanie realised the doubt must have shown on her face.

'When did he say that? We didn't see him yesterday — not to speak to, anyway.' Tiphanie had made sure of that. Instead of the local swimming baths, she'd taken the twins to another sports centre. The three of them had made use of all of the amenities, and hadn't returned until quite late in the evening.

'He said it when we saw him at the station while you were giving Tad what for, and again when we fetched Marmaduke and Crystal out of his garden,' Jack told her.

'I suppose you can go, then,'

Tiphanie replied, trying not to wince at the memory of what had happened when they'd gone to fetch the cats. 'Be back for one o'clock, though, I've planned a special meal. And make sure Duke and Crystal don't follow you,' she yelled as the two of them dashed out.

She glanced at the clock. If she lit the barbecue now, she'd have time to do an hour's work while the charcoal was heating up. She'd put chicken wings and steak to marinate and prepared a salad earlier on while Jack and Zoe were packing their things.

'But first, I'll just go and watch through the binoculars to make sure Jack and Zoe get there safely,' she murmured as she sped up the twisty staircase to the studio. Huh, who was she kidding? She was desperate for a glimpse of Kyle. She hadn't seen him since yesterday morning.

However, all she saw was the twins knocking on the front door and then going into the cottage. 'Kyle must have called out for them to go in.' She sighed in frustration.

*   *   *

'Hello, you two,' Kyle said, glancing up from his laptop. 'Sit down and hang on a minute, I just want to finish this chapter.'

When he'd saved his work and looked up again, he saw Zoe was glancing with a strange look on her face at his 4-in-1 music system, where a vinyl record of Handel's *Water Music* was playing. 'Don't look so surprised,' he said. 'I do like background music while I work; but, unlike someone we all know, I only have it on very low.'

'It's what the record is, not because you're playing one,' Jack said.

'I've a few CDs and records with this piece on,' Kyle told him, walking over to the couch. 'But this orchestra's rendition of it is one of the best I've ever heard.'

'It's our mum's orchestra,' Zoe said,

smiling up at him.

'You what, Zoe?' Kyle couldn't quite work out what she meant.

'Mum's conducting the orchestra,' Jack explained. He reached for the nearby record sleeve. 'See, here's her name: Fiona West Timpson.'

'You . . . Your . . . ' His mind spun with bewilderment as a gamut of perplexing emotions chased through it. 'Did you say Fiona Timpson is your mother?'

'We told you, we live with our gran because Mum works away a lot,' Zoe reminded him. 'She travels all over the world with the orchestra. It's quite a famous one, you know. When Daddy was killed in the plane crash, with his mum, our other grandma . . . ' Zoe gulped before continuing. ' . . . well, Mum was ill for quite a while . . . '

Her eyes clouded and she reached for her twin's hand. In spite of most of his mind being taken up with wondering how the hell he could have got things so wrong, Kyle wanted to reach out and hug the little girl.

But it was Jack who turned to give her a quick cuddle before taking over the sad story in a gruff voice. 'Then everybody, Tiphanie, Tad, Tristan — Daddy was Tris's twin — and Grandad Timpson and Grandma West — '

'Our mum was her daughter,' Zoe interrupted.

Jack nodded. 'They all persuaded Mum to go back to work. They said there were more than enough of them to look after us when she had to go abroad. Only it's Tiphanie who always ends up with us if Gran wants a break or has to go into hospital or anything.'

'She's been in hospital this week,' said Zoe. 'Well, only for two days, but Tiphanie told her to go away on holiday for the rest of the week. And Tristan said we could come to his place.'

'But Tris played a dirty trick really,' said Jack. 'He said he'd like Tiphanie to come and help him give us a good time, but really he wanted her here so she could look after his cat because he needed to go somewhere for a few days.'

'And Tiphanie cancelled a proper holiday to bring us here,' said Zoe. 'She always lets her brothers do things like that. Last time Mum was home, she said it was no wonder Tiphanie had never married because no man in their right mind would put up with her dropping everything the second her brothers asked her to do anything. I won't let Jack do it to me when we're grown up.'

'So ... so Tristan is Tiphanie's *brother*,' Kyle said, aware his voice had risen on that last word.

'Of course he is,' Jack said. 'He's our uncle, but we hardly ever call him Uncle Tristan. We don't call Tad uncle, either. He's Tiphanie's twin. I don't know why we've got so many twins but we have.'

If only they did call Tad 'uncle', I wouldn't have thought Zoe was calling him 'Dad' whenever she mentioned him — or jumped to the conclusion he was

Tiphanie's ex-husband, Kyle thought bleakly.

'You saw Tiphanie arguing with Tad at the station,' said Zoe. 'Didn't you notice how alike they are? It's funny really, 'cos we look like them, but our daddy and Tristan were almost identical twins, and . . .'

Kyle couldn't hide his despair and horror any longer. He buried his face in his hands. God, what had he done? He'd thought . . . He'd accused . . . He groaned his torment aloud.

'Kyle, whatever's wrong? Has it upset you hearing about our mum and our grandma? It still upsets us sometimes, even though it was five years ago; but we still talk about both of them because it would make us sadder not to.' Zoe moved from the couch and went to kneel before his chair. 'Should Jack run and fetch Tiphanie?' she asked gently stroking his hands.

'After the things I said to your *aunt* and the way I've behaved towards her, she'll probably never speak to me again.

I thought Tiphanie . . . ' Kyle stopped suddenly. There was no way he could tell Jack and Zoe what he'd thought, what he'd accused Tiphanie of. He still couldn't work out the wedding ring bit, but clearly he'd got that completely wrong as well.

Lowering his hands, he gazed at Zoe. 'Promise me you will never accuse anyone of anything until you're sure of all your facts,' he said. 'Otherwise, you'll end up hurting.'

'If you said something wrong to Tiphanie, all you have to do is go and say you're sorry.' Zoe looked earnestly at him. 'Tiphanie often loses her temper and says horrible things, things she doesn't really mean, but afterwards she's sorry. She'll understand exactly how you feel, Kyle.'

'It's artistic temperament. That's what Gran West calls it,' Jack mumbled, looking up from a book he'd taken off one of the bookcase shelves. 'I bet you have to make yourself feel angry sometimes when you're writing about cowboys having gunfights. Especially if you're writing in Spanish. This is Spanish, isn't it?'

Kyle forced a smile as he explained that he wrote his stories in English, and then they were translated into other languages. He pointed to a photograph on the sideboard. 'Dee-Dee translates some of them for me. She's a very special person; maybe you'll meet her one day.'

'Did you dedicate this book to her?' Jack asked. 'I saw her name at the front.' He flicked back a few pages. 'Here. What does it mean in English, Kyle?'

'"To the one and only Dee-Dee", or words to that effect,' Kyle replied absent-mindedly, his thoughts very much elsewhere.

Zoe scrambled up, walked over to pick up the photograph, then wandered to the window with it. 'I thought so. This photo was taken over there, just past the bridge. Oh, look,' she added as she started to turn away, 'there are two cars driving up to Tristan's. I wonder who's in them.'

Jack joined her at the window. 'The first car is Tad's, I think. Maybe he's brought their house-guests to see the place. Herr Meier said they'd love to see it when we showed them the picture of the lighthouse in our book and told them the old smock mill looked a bit like it. Can I use these binoculars, Kyle?'

Kyle nodded.

'Is it Tad, Jack?' Zoe asked impatiently.

'Yes. Here, have a look.' Jack passed her the binoculars, but Zoe stepped over to Kyle and pushed them into his hands.

'You come and look, Kyle. Tiphanie is sure to run out when she hears the cars, and when you see her and Tad together, you'll see how alike they are.'

Unable to think of a reason for refusing, Kyle did as Zoe said. His heart lurched and his knuckles tightened uncomfortably as he trained the binoculars onto the door of Marsh View.

Yes, there was Tiphanie, orange hair flaming in the sunlight, one hand full of skewers as she leapt down the four steps to go and greet her guests. He watched Tad get out of the car, saw him laughing as he spoke to her, and then she was surrounded by the people from the second car and he couldn't see her any more.

'You two had better go,' he said, lowering the binoculars and hoping that the twins wouldn't comment on how husky his voice had been.

'Why don't you come with us?' Jack suggested. 'It looks like there's going to be a party. I'm sure Linda and Tad are getting a hamper out of the car boot.'

'I've got to go out,' Kyle said truthfully. 'I'm seeing Dee-Dee. I turn my hand to a spot of cartography sometimes, and we're working on a map for the endpapers of a new book.' He didn't think he'd get much done with his mind on how badly he'd misjudged Tiphanie, but it wouldn't be fair to cancel his meeting with Dee-Dee.

'Well, maybe we'll see you next time we visit.' Zoe scrambled onto the couch and, standing, leaned over the back of it and put her arms around Kyle's neck. 'Don't worry about whatever you said to Tiphanie,' she whispered. 'She'll forgive you, I know she will. She watched you jogging yesterday, and she looked all sad and . . . and *wistful*.'

She's got a helluva lot to forgive, Kyle thought as he ruffled Zoe's hair before lifting her down to the floor. And, after shaking hands with Jack and giving him a gentle thump on the shoulder, he stood in the doorway, inwardly hollow, and watched them go.

* * *

It was five o'clock when Tiphanie's unexpected guests departed; though, to make up for descending upon her, Tad offered to take Jack and Zoe back to their gran's. She agreed readily; she couldn't wait to be on her own to think about what Zoe had hurriedly told her when they'd been feeding the cats together: 'Kyle's very upset about something he said to you. I think he'll be coming to see you soon to ask you to forgive him.'

There hadn't been time for more, as Linda and Tad had come into the kitchen and Zoe started chattering about something else.

Now, Tiphanie closed the gate after the cars had driven through, and waved until they were out of sight. Glad she was wearing a long sweater because there was a cool breeze, she turned and wandered slowly back along the river bank to Marsh View, Zoe's words ringing in her ears. I suppose he wants to apologise for calling me deceitful, she mused. Or maybe he's realised Tristan is my brother, not 'one of my men'. Yes, that'll be it. I expect the twins said something and the penny dropped.

She supposed she should forgive him for thinking that. After all, she hadn't said anything to enlighten him. Quite the reverse: she'd actually played up to it. She'd encouraged him to think Tris and her . . .

She stopped dead and felt her face flaming with anger. She had tried to tell him the truth that night Howard called. Look where it had got her. Kyle-Mr-Sarky-Cooper had as good as called her promiscuous. If he thought he could beg forgiveness for that, he'd got another think coming. She'd never forgive him. Never.

All the hurt she'd felt that night came flooding back, serving to strengthen her resolve. She recalled, too, how when she and the twins had gone to get the cats out of his garden, he'd shown nothing but anger and scorn. He'd even told her she was beneath all contempt.

So, no, she wouldn't forgive him: she wouldn't even think about him again; she'd put him right out of her mind. She stared moodily into the river.

Watching water was supposed to be soothing, wasn't it?

Nothing would soothe her chained memories, she acknowledged as she started to walk again. She might be able to put him out of her mind for a while, but not out of her heart. He was there all the time.

A few minutes later, Kyle was in her sight too. He was driving along on the other side of the river bank towards his cottage. Tiphanie forced herself to look down into the river, but she could feel his eyes burning into her. It was almost as though he were holding her, and her lips tingled in remembrance of his kiss.

She heard his car screech to a halt, followed by the slamming of a door, and then she heard him call her name. She glanced quickly across to the other side, saw him running back towards the bridge, and knew she had to get away . . . had to go somewhere he wouldn't follow. She wasn't ready to face him. If Zoe was right and he wanted to apologise for something he'd said

— whichever of his barbs it was — she wanted to feel cool and calm and not plagued by memories of the gentle Kyle who'd looked after her after her fall from the tree.

The tree . . . She'd climb to the top. OK, so maybe she was behaving childishly, but he wouldn't follow her there.

★ ★ ★

But within minutes of her reaching the top of the tree, Kyle appeared on the branch below her. 'Why did you let me think Jack and Zoe were your children?' he demanded, grabbing hold of one of her ankles and shaking it. 'Why, Tiphanie?'

So much for Zoe thinking Kyle wanted to apologise — to ask for forgiveness. He just wanted to hurl more insults. Furious at herself for not pulling her ankle away sooner, for allowing his fingers to linger there, she tried fruitlessly to get free.

'Let go of me, Kyle. I don't know what you're talking about. OK, I admit I let Angus Gilbert think the twins were mine whenever I went to the magazine publishers, but I don't see how you could have thought so.'

He let go of her ankle to answer harshly, 'One, they look like you. Two, I heard you more than once telling Zoe not to call you 'Mum'. Three — '

'Don't be so ridiculous.' Regardless of any danger — and anyway, her anger overrode any other feeling — Tiphanie jumped down onto the branch Kyle was standing on. 'I can't help it if they look like me. That doesn't make other people — *normal* people — think they're mine. And I have never told Zoe not to call me 'Mum'. How could I have done? She's perfectly aware of who her mother is.

'You honestly mean to say you thought Jack and Zoe were my children, but I wouldn't allow them to call me Mum? And who was their father supposed to have been? Oh, I get it. You thought I was married or separated, but playing around. When you saw me wearing my mum's wedding band on my wedding finger, you thought I was trying to get money out of the twins' father, taking him for a 'poor sucker' while all the time I was earning a good living as well as having umpteen men in my life to pay for things.'

Fully wound up now, Tiphanie hardly paused to take breath before continuing: 'You thought I had Howard, Tristan and Dave on a string, seeing all three of them — and more than seeing, that's what you thought, isn't it? You're so bitter and twisted about your own failed marriage and your own ex-wife that you can't see or think straight. It must hurt like hell having all that bitterness inside you. It must — '

There was an ominous crack as the branch they were both standing on broke. Tiphanie managed to break her fall by catching hold of another branch. Kyle was still on the remaining part of the broken one. She heard him say her name, a strangled sound from deep in his throat. Her anger fled immediately, her anxiety for him taking over.

Staring up, she could see the sweat on his brow and upper lip; his face was green-tinged and she knew it wasn't a reflection from the leaves. She noted his whitened knuckles as he clung onto a branch above his head. She had never suffered from height vertigo, but she did know what fear felt like.

She swarmed up until she was just below the broken branch. 'Kyle,' she said firmly. 'Stop looking down and concentrate only on my voice. I'm going to hold your feet and guide them down branch by branch. You'll have to help me, Kyle. Help me and trust me.'

It seemed to take forever. Tiphanie kept on talking soothingly all the time; she didn't dare look down herself, she had to concentrate as she moved Kyle's feet slowly, so slowly, from branch to branch. Her mouth went dry and she held her breath as one of his hands slipped off a branch. His whole body swayed and she thought he'd fall, but somehow he found a handhold. She was trembling with relief and from her own effort to stay calm.

She felt her knees brush past the tree-house and gulped thankfully. 'Two more branches down, and the top half of your body will be level with the tree-house, Kyle. Wiggle into it: I'll push your legs in.' She felt the extra tenseness in him. 'I'll be right with you. We need a rest. You'll have to do it.'

Sending up a silent prayer, Tiphanie watched him fumble the top half of his body into the wooden structure, and from somewhere found the extra strength to manoeuvre his legs to her right and swing them upwards.

And, at last, he was safely in.

Kyle was lying on his back on the floor of the tree-house, his eyes tightly shut, his jaw clenched, and she could see his whole body shaking with reaction as she wriggled in beside him. Warmth was supposed to be good for shock, wasn't it? She needed something to cover him with. But what?

There was only one thing for it. She pulled off her sweater and put it over him, tucking it underneath his body wherever she could; then, kneeling across him, she smoothed his hair from his face.

'I'm cold,' he muttered. 'So cold.'

Tiphanie took one of his hands and, holding it between hers, rubbed it. It felt like a block of ice so she rubbed a bit harder.

'Hold me, Tiphanie. Hold me until I can stop this damned shaking.'

She lay on top of him, holding him close, pressing herself into him to share her warmth.

When Kyle eventually opened his eyes, Tiphanie looked deep into them and recognised she was caught in the grip of destiny. He'd stopped shivering and now she was aware of heat beating through his body. Aware, too, of the frantic thudding of her heart as he pulled her even closer to him. The sound of their harsh breathing echoed around the planked walls as they gazed into each other's eyes.

Then his lips captured hers, caressing her mouth more than kissing it, and she quivered at the sweet tenderness. Feather-kisses, as light as a summer breeze, turned into one long kiss for her soul to melt into. His lips left hers to nibble at her earlobe before recapturing her mouth.

Now there was a dreamy intimacy to their kiss, and she felt as though she was floating on a soft and wispy cloud. A moan of ecstasy slipped through her lips and a delicious shudder heated her body as his fingers played over her bare shoulders. He moved, pulling her underneath him.

But then she was falling. She called his name aloud — in a protest, a plea, a prayer, she knew not what. All she knew was that she was being denied his touch. She landed with a thud that drove all remaining breath from her body. She lay there for a while before sitting up gingerly and saw Kyle was sitting on the ground next to her, his head between his knees, breathing harshly. 'Are you all right?' she whispered. 'Kyle, speak to me.' She crawled over to him and forced his head up.

'Tiphanie,' he gasped. 'Next time we want to . . . need to . . . Next time we decide we'll get to know each other better, for God's sake let's not do it in a tree-house.'

'Next time you build a tree-house, make it stronger,' she returned, laughing in attempt to hide her true feelings: a mixture of sorrow and gladness. She knew under normal circumstances she'd never allow things to go any further than they had — not with so many misunderstandings between them — not until she knew there was more than just desire between them. But if the tree-house hadn't collapsed when it did . . .

Well, she wasn't sure she'd have been able to take either of those things into account. Who was she kidding? She *knew* she wouldn't have done so. Hence the feeling of sorrow; it was for what might have been.

Her thoughts and meanderings came to a startling halt as she recalled taking her sweater off to wrap around him, and remembered that the only thing covering her top half was a lacy and very sheer camisole halter top.

She got to her feet abruptly, wincing as her bruises made themselves felt. And when she noticed her sweater hanging over the lower branches of the tree, she had to stem her almost hysterical laughter. If Jack and Zoe were here, they'd start a game of Connections, and the connections would be Enid Blyton's 'Faraway Tree' stories and Dame Washalot hanging washing over branches to dry. The only connection she thought fit, though, was 'airing one's dirty linen in public'.

As she stretched up to get her sweater, Kyle's voice came from behind her. 'Allow me,' he said.

His body brushed hers as he reached

up, and new frissons of awareness ran through her. But the mocking tone had been back in his voice and she guessed he was regretting their earlier closeness. Just as she should be, she told herself.

'I've still got some explaining to do, and so have you,' he said harshly as he handed her the sweater. 'I'll go home and have a shower, and then I'll come back, Tiphanie. No running off, no trying to hide this time. You owe it to me to let me explain.'

'Of all the — ' Tiphanie began, but he interrupted.

'You might like to put your sweater back on,' he said provokingly. 'People sometimes take a walk down here on a pleasant spring evening.'

'You're insufferable, Kyle-Mr-Sarky-Cooper,' she called over her shoulder. And his mocking laughter followed her as she sprinted towards Marsh View.

'I won't do any explaining when he comes back,' she told Crystal and Marmaduke who were sitting on the steps up to the front door. 'I don't owe him *anything*. He can't just order me around like that.'

But deep down, she knew she wanted to explain — and listen to his explanations, too.

10

In the early-evening twilight, as though uncertain of its welcome, the reflection of the moon trembled shyly on the sleepy waters of the meandering river. On the river bank, a heron, tall and majestic, stared steadfastly down at the elusive image. From the gently swaying water reeds, the sweet silvery voice of a reed warbler carolled its last song of the day, ingeniously applauded by the hidden gathering of frogs croaking to each other as they settled in their secret riverside resting places.

The very evocativeness took on the guise of a mesmerist pulling at the heartstrings — causing Kyle to pause on the bridge to immerse his soul in the serenity.

★　★　★

Tiphanie threw a shawl over her shoulders before stepping back outside to move swiftly but silently towards the bridge. She knew that, whatever spectres of the past lay between them, she had to share this poignant beauty with Kyle.

He seemed to sense her arrival as though he'd been waiting for her, as though he were testing her willingness to let him explain his misunderstandings of her. He put his arm around her shoulders and drew her close.

Their lips met unerringly: a gentle, kind, soothing kiss, its poignancy matching that of the evening's. Any lingering anger and hurt Tiphanie might have been harbouring fled. She felt as if she'd come home, as if she'd found the beginning of the rest of her life.

Eventually, the reed warbler's heartbreaking melody ceased, the heron winged its way home and the frogs' croaking became infrequent. 'Do you know your Shakespeare?' Kyle spoke softly as if he was afraid to break the enchantment still surrounding them.

You've got golden flecks in your eyes, was Tiphanie's silent reply as she gazed upwards, though her mouth formed the words, 'I should do. Jack and Zoe devour his works.'

'Falstaff spoke about the drone of a Lincolnshire bagpipe — '

'In part one of *Henry IV*.'

'That's right. The question being, what is a Lincolnshire bagpipe?' Featherlike laugh lines crinkled around his eyes as he looked down at her, and she wanted to reach up and touch his face.

Stepping away slightly, she said, 'I don't know. You'll have to tell me.'

'Falstaff was referring to the croaking of frogs.'

His smile sent her pulse racing and, dragging her eyes away from his face, she said, 'I must remember that next time I play Connections with the twins. I'll ask them to connect one of Balfe's operas to a frog — or maybe to connect *The Merry Wives of Windsor* to one, because Balfe based his *Falstaff* on that.' Tiphanie knew she was burbling, preventing the words she really wanted to say from escaping.

She wanted to ask him to hold her, to love her, to . . . Spotting Tristan's cat strolling towards them, she heaved a sigh of relief for the distraction. Bending, she held out a hand and crooned, 'Come on, Mum . . . sorry, I mean Crystal.'

'*That's* it,' Kyle said. 'That's what made me think you were the twins' mother. Zoe kept calling you 'Mum' and then apologising.'

Tiphanie heard him drumming his fingers on the bridge's rail, and guessed he was probably trying to recall the times Zoe had done that.

'When you woke up from sleeping off your fright after falling from the tree, Zoe ran over to the bed and said: 'Mum — sorry, Tiphanie' . . . She said it at other times, too.'

Crystal, as though aware she'd lost Tiphanie's attention, wandered off, and

Tiphanie turned to face Kyle. 'You got it wrong,' she said. 'Zoe kept calling Tristan's *cat* 'Mum'. You see, she used to be called Chrysanthe*mum*, and she had kittens and we shortened her name to 'Mum'. But then . . . '

Tiphanie went on to explain about the cat therapist and how Tristan, on her advice, had started calling his cat Crystal and insisted everyone else did, too. 'And since we're talking of Tristan, I can understand how you got the wrong idea about him and me. When you first saw us together, I suppose to you, he didn't seem to be acting in a brotherly manner. But I was writhing in agony, not with desire. I'd got some skin caught in my zip — '

'I have noticed you wear jeans with a zip up the back,' Kyle commented dryly.

She chose to ignore his interruption and went on, 'I was so annoyed by your derogatory manner, I decided to let you continue thinking that Tris was . . . That Tristan and I were . . . '

'That you were rather more than just good friends.' Kyle nodded. 'I thought *then* that you'd come from being more than good friends with Howard straight to Tristan. And then Tristan went away leaving you at his place, and another man appeared on the scene a couple of hours after.'

'Dave,' Tiphanie said with a sigh.

'And I saw him wearing nothing but a towel. I met him the other day when he was with his wife. They soon made me realise I'd made a terrible mistake and that, in that instance, I had judged you wrongly.'

'Dave is one of Tristan's oldest friends. We've both known him for ages. He's like another brother to me.'

'I know that now. I also know . . . ' He ran his fingers through his hair, and Tiphanie knew he was wondering how to continue. 'I also know what really happened between you and Howard,' he said at last.

Not touching her, not looking at her, he stared down into the river as he told her about phoning her the night of her fall. 'You started yelling the minute you picked up the phone because you thought it was Howard, and I . . . I just listened,' he confessed.

'So who out of Tristan, Dave and Howard did you have down as the twins' father before you found out the truth?' she asked with remarkable self-control.

'Someone else entirely,' he replied ruefully. 'Again, it was Zoe who made me think so. I suppose it's unfair blaming her, but it was the way she talked about Tad. I thought she was calling him 'Dad', you see. And — '

Suddenly, now Kyle knew the truth, Tiphanie saw the funny side of things. 'It's like a third-rate farce,' she gasped, laughter bubbling up. 'With me playing the leading role as a scarlet woman.'

But, just as suddenly, she sobered. 'Even before you knew the truth, you kissed me. Have you read *The Book of the It* where Georg Groddeck stated, 'Do not wonder at the man who runs after a heartless coquette, but keep your wonder for the man who does not'?'

Clearly surprised at her swing of mood, Kyle groaned. 'I can't apologise for any of the times I kissed you. But surely you realise I didn't exactly plan for what almost happened in the tree-house today?'

'Well, *that* bit sounds like an apology,' Tiphanie snapped, the thought hurting her.

He shook his head in denial. 'It seemed so right, so natural, so *meant*. I can't promise something like that won't happen again. There's been some kind of feeling between us right from the start. We can't just discard it or ignore it. Oh, I tried to, especially when I thought your behaviour reminded me of my ex-wife. But even then I wanted to . . . '

'Wanted to what?' she asked softly.

'I don't know. Trust you, I suppose. The way Denise behaved tarnished me. I find it hard to trust any woman. You have to trust before you can love. Could we start over, do you think? See where the feeling will take us. Cherish it, mature it, and allow it to grow slowly but surely.'

He put his hands on her shoulders and looked down into her eyes. 'You quoted Georg Groddeck. Let me quote Oscar Wilde: 'When you really want love you will find it waiting for you'. Shall we see if it's waiting for us, Tiphanie?'

He didn't wait for any response; lowering his head, he dropped a light butterfly kiss on the tip of her nose. 'I've got an appointment on Tuesday, but why don't we play hooky tomorrow? We could set out at dawn and I'll take you to Cambridge for the day. Show you some of my favourite places. What do you think?'

'I think I'd like that,' she replied breathlessly, not sure which of his words she was replying to.

'In that case, if you're ready to go back in now, I'll walk with you and then go home to do some work.'

He kept one arm around her as they sauntered slowly and silently over the bridge and along the river bank towards Marsh View. At the steps, he brushed a finger down her cheek before turning to make his way to his cottage.

Crystal and Marmaduke appeared from somewhere and wound themselves round Tiphanie's legs. But Tiphanie stayed where she was, hand up to her cheek, and watched until he was a shadow in the dusk on the other side of the river. She saw him raise his hand, and that wave kindled a feeling of contentment which she carried inside with her.

Followed by the cats, she hurried up to the studio to work. Knowing Kyle was working too somehow made it seem as though they were still together.

'And it seems likely Kyle and I might be together quite a bit,' she said, rubbing Marmaduke's head. 'Hopefully we'll get him to start liking cats, hmm?'

* * *

At five o'clock the next morning, Tiphanie smiled mischievously to herself as she punched out Kyle's number. 'Is this dawn enough for you?' she asked. 'I thought you might like to come for breakfast. I'm famous for my 'mixie-medley'.'

'Sounds irresistible.' His throaty reply sent delicate shivers of delight down Tiphanie's spine. 'How long will it take you to prepare such a delicacy?'

'Give me twenty minutes. You haven't even asked what it is,' she added.

'I love early-morning surprises. And I'll be there on time.'

'See you soon, then,' Tiphanie said, ending the call.

* * *

'I just hope my surprise breakfast isn't too filling,' Kyle muttered as he resumed the task Tiphanie's phone call had interrupted, washing up his breakfast things

265

— he'd already eaten a hearty meal of eggs, bacon, mushrooms and tomatoes.

A few minutes later the phone rang again. 'Um, Kyle, I don't suppose you've got any eggs?' was the plaintive query. 'I've only got one left. I'd forgotten I made pancakes for eight people yesterday.'

'Sorry, I haven't.' Kyle couldn't hide his laughter.

'It isn't funny. I can't make mixie-medley without at least three eggs. I've got cream, ham, cheese and tomatoes . . . that's what goes in it, you see. It's a sort of glorified scrambled eggs. Stop laughing, Kyle.'

'How about if you make something just for yourself, and I'll come over and share your coffee. I'd already eaten when you phoned the first time, only I didn't want to miss out on the chance of breakfasting with you,' he confessed, and was pleased when Tiphanie's giggling came down the line.

'I'll boil my one egg, make some toast, and put the coffee on to percolate,' she said. 'I like using a percolator more than a cafetière.'

'Me too,' he agreed. 'See you soon.'

Tiphanie hummed happily as she made her own breakfast. She was so looking forward to spending the whole day with him.

11

'Next time we decide to come to Cambridge we'll have to hire a cabin cruiser.' Kyle sighed with relief as he parked his car in the multi-storey car park. 'It really is an unpleasant journey by road. No matter what time of day it is, it's always busy.'

'Never mind, we'll enjoy it now we're here,' consoled Tiphanie. 'Though I always think you need a few weeks to see everything.'

Kyle stopped in the act of opening his car door. 'Do you know Cambridge well?' he asked suspiciously.

'Can one ever know it well?' Tiphanie fiddled with her door handle to try and avoid looking at him, not willing to admit that a couple of years ago, Tristan and her father had taken part in the Annual Summer School held at St John's College. Her father, knowing he wouldn't be able to see everything he wanted to during those two weeks, had installed Tiphanie in a rented cottage in Grantchester for a month, joining her there after his session at the Summer School.

As Tristan's girlfriend of that time also happened to live in the village, Tiphanie had been lucky enough to have an excellent guide, and they'd explored Cambridge and its outlying areas thoroughly.

'How well do you know it, Tiphanie? You don't live here, do you?'

'No. But I do know it well enough to look forward to reacquainting myself with the colleges, the gardens, the libraries, the walks, the . . . ' She broke off, realising her enthusiasm had given her away. Laughing, she added, 'Like you and breakfast this morning, I didn't want to miss out on the chance of coming with you.

'Besides, it was summer when I came. We spent a month here steeping ourselves in history. I've never been here in springtime, though. Everything will look different.' And seeing it with you will be something to treasure, she added silently as they got out of the car.

★ ★ ★

Just as silently, Kyle wondered who Tiphanie had spent that month with. He wanted to give her new memories, not resurrect old ones.

'I came with Tristan and my father last time,' she said, as though she'd read his mind.

'Where shall we go first?' he asked. And he was aware his voice was husky with relief.

'You were going to show me your favourite places,' she reminded him. 'But I would like to visit Christ's College. Hopefully, we'll be allowed in the Fellows' Garden.'

'I might have guessed that. You want to see 'Milton's Mulberry Tree'. I wonder if he really wrote 'Lycidas' whilst sitting under it.'

'For someone who writes Westerns, you've got a surprisingly classical mind,' teased Tiphanie.

'I could say the same of a certain cartoonist,' he returned, laughing. 'I never did get to 'see your etchings', did I? You'll have to introduce me to your cartoon family soon. Do you get your ideas from everyday happenings? I know I do.'

'What? How can you get ideas for cowboys and Indians from everyday happenings?' she asked, standing still and looking up at him in amazement.

He took her hand and they started walking again. 'I write short stories as well,' he explained. 'I really wanted to become known for that. I can't remember a time I didn't want to be an author. I was rather like the twins when I was young; I devoured Shakespeare and the classics and anything else I could get my hands on.

'When I was in my late teens, I had a long bout of illness. I used to watch television a lot — there were always

Westerns on in the afternoon, and I decided to have a go at writing one. I finished it, stashed it away, and forgot all about it. Then, a few years ago, when I was making a mediocre living from my short stories, my agent asked me if I'd try my hand at a Western.'

'So you dug out the one you'd written years before from under your bed, wiped off the dust-bunnies, and gave it to your agent to read?' Tiphanie said with a smile.

Kyle nodded. 'It was accepted, the publisher wanted more, and after a couple of years America and Spain started to buy the rights. But I still harbour a dream of becoming known for a more literary style of writing. Especially when I visit Cambridge. Have you seen the Pepys Library, Tiphanie?'

★　★　★

'Yes, and I loved it. Can we make time to go today?' Her intuition told her that it was one of Kyle's favourite places — she suddenly seemed to have learned so much about him in a short space of time. Maybe they would have a chance to build future dreams together, she thought, and smiled up at him.

They discovered such a lot in common as they wandered happily around from college to college. Tiphanie felt as though she'd found her soulmate at last. She remembered how she'd thought once before that Kyle was a missing part of her. The part to make her complete. And she'd been right.

'Do you know Wordsworth's *The Prelude*?' Kyle asked softly as they stood side by side in the cold, white chamber in the antechapel belonging to Trinity College. 'He wrote about this statue of Newton. I love the line: 'Voyaging through strange seas of Thought, alone'. But I don't think I want to voyage alone.'

'He mentions the clock in the clock-tower as well,' whispered Tiphanie. She felt somewhat overawed by the statues that dominated the antechapel. Over-awed, too, at her depth of love for Kyle. She knew now she really did love him — with an almost frightening intensity.

A short while later, near the area known as 'Mutton-Hole Corner', she was laughing as Kyle intoned solemnly, 'This is where Lord Byron used to keep his tame bear. They weren't allowed to keep dogs,' he added to a tourist who looked rather puzzled on hearing about the bear. 'Legend has it that Byron was sent down. Not for keeping the bear, but . . . ' He lowered his voice dramatically. ' . . . for bathing naked in the fountain.'

'Kyle, stop it,' Tiphanie said, laughing as an interested audience began to applaud softly. She misquoted from Rupert Brooke's famous poem about Grantchester, 'Let's go for a walk across the meadows to a certain place where the church clock used to stand at ten to three, and we'll see if we can find some honey for our tea.'

'All this culture and she wants food.'

Kyle shrugged and made a mock bow to the small crowd before drawing her away. 'Surely you'd like to visit the Fitzwilliam Museum?' he asked.

'Too much to see and not enough time to see it. If the *choice* is mine, before we eat we could explore around Trumpington Street.'

She was throwing out a challenge and Kyle rose to it. 'You want to see a certain monument.' Chuckling, he pretended to be reading from an imaginary book. 'Thomas Hobson, many times Mayor of Cambridge, once owned a livery stable. However, if one wanted to hire one of his horses, they had to take the animal nearest the door, and not necessarily the animal of their choice.' So . . . '

Kyle closed the imaginary book and, turning, kissed Tiphanie's ear before whispering in it, 'So, you are presenting me with Hobson's Choice. We'll go and explore Trumpington Street and all things Hobson, and after that we'll have afternoon tea.'

After they'd seen all they wanted to, they retraced their steps and made their way towards the bar and brasserie with, Kyle told her, a fantastic and unusual afternoon tea menu. His arm was around her waist, casually encircling it as they walked, and the touch of his hand was almost unbearable in its tenderness. A primitive yearning sparkled into life and her breath came in uneven gasps.

'Am I walking too quickly for you?' He slowed his pace and turned his head to look down at her. She saw him catch his breath as his eyes met hers; licking her dry lips, she watched his pupils darken.

'I don't know about a cup of tea, I think I need an iced drink to cool my thoughts,' he added. His voice was grained and earthy, husky and disjointed, and he smiled wryly at her.

She nodded and smiled and didn't know whether she was glad or sorry when they arrived.

It was warm enough to sit outside on the terrace, and again Tiphanie saw how much they had in common after a selection of finger sandwiches arrived and they both decided that the lobster with a delicious herby mayonnaise was their favourite.

They differed on the scones, though. Tiphanie went for a fruit one and Kyle a plain. But they both had strawberry jam and clotted cream. True to his word, Kyle had ordered an iced tea, while Tiphanie decided to try one known as 'Blend 1886'.

'Hobson's monument was erected in eighteen-sixty something. So,' she said, laughing, 'this blend of tea is the nearest I can get to anything Hobson.'

Will I be faced with 'Hobson's Choice' when we get home? Tiphanie wondered. What if Kyle suggests us spending the night together? The thought both excited and frightened her. Frightened her because she loved him so deeply, but didn't know if he loved her — excited her because she knew the way his touch could make her feel.

Meeting his eyes across the table, she had a strong feeling he was having the same erotic thoughts . . .

★　★　★

They hardly spoke on the way home; it was a tranquil, expectant journey. Tiphanie dreamily watched Kyle's competence at the wheel, remembering the touch of his hands on her body when they'd been in the tree-house and how his body had felt.

Kyle whistled softly as he drove and recognising the tune, Tiphanie murmured, 'Debussy's 'Sounds and fragrances swirl in the evening air'.'

'Debussy's *Préludes* are one of my passions,' he said, glancing at her briefly but meaningfully.

As he resumed whistling, Tiphanie hummed companionably along under her breath while thinking, *this* is a prelude to passion. This being here together, travelling together, is just the beginning of the journey we're going to make.

She wondered if they'd go to Marsh View or to his cottage. She'd never seen inside his home, never seen where he sat, where he ate, where he worked, where he slept. A frisson of awareness flickered through her at the thought of Kyle's bed, and she was glad he had his eyes on the road; she was sure he'd be able to sense her inner excitement if he looked at her.

* * *

Kyle's eyes might have been on the road, but his thoughts weren't just on his driving. He couldn't wait to get home. He wanted to take Tiphanie to his cottage and show her his bathroom. It had been installed by the previous owner, and he'd always felt slightly embarrassed about it until now. It was an erotic room with a huge air bath, full-length mirrors, and also a ceiling mirror.

'It's at times like this I wish I smoked,' he muttered as his body reacted violently to his thoughts. 'I want you in my arms, and this journey is taking far too long.'

'I was thinking exactly the same,' she told him. 'Not the smoking bit, the rest of it.'

'That's good, because it takes two to tango,' he said. 'Not a particularly loving response, I know. But a loving response would only have made me want you more, and I want to get us home safely.'

*   *   *

Tiphanie closed her eyes and let her mind drift, secretly revelling in the intensity of Kyle's words. But mixed with her euphoria was apprehension. Apprehension about how they'd feel afterwards — if they made love. Would Kyle's feelings for her deepen, as hers undoubtedly would for him? Would making love make him love her?

Only if he can find it in his heart to trust you, warned her inner voice. Kyle must learn to trust before he'll allow himself to truly love.

I'll teach him to trust, Tiphanie vowed. Trust every word, every glance, every action, every feeling between us. I wonder what his ex-wife did to betray his trust. I suppose he *has* stopped loving her? Yes, he must have done; he certainly doesn't trust her.

But does it work that way round? He won't love me until he trusts me, but he once trusted and loved Denise. Just because she betrayed his trust doesn't mean she destroyed his love, does it? Yes, of course it does. Heck, I was so happy before I started thinking like this. Why have I suddenly let all these doubts creep in?

It was because she'd had time to think. If only they could have made love after one of their shared magnetic moments instead of having to drive home. It wouldn't seem natural now; it just seemed planned in advance.

She opened her eyes and glanced out of the window. They hadn't far to go now, and she needed something to reassure her before they arrived. Before they . . .

'How long have you lived in your cottage, Kyle?' she asked, knowing from what Tristan had said that Denise had never lived there with Kyle. What she was really trying to work out was how long Kyle had been divorced. She knew, again from what Tristan had told her, that Denise had tried to get more money out of Kyle when his Westerns had become so sought after, and Kyle himself had said that Spain and America had started buying the rights a couple of years ago.

'I've lived there about six months.' Kyle glanced quickly at her, clearly surprised by her seemingly irrelevant question. Perhaps he was aware of her doubts, though, because he added huskily, 'Having second thoughts?

Nothing will happen unless you want it to, Tiphanie.'

Suddenly everything was all right again. His husky tone and his awareness of her doubts showed he cared. And they were driving along the track to his cottage now. Once she was in his arms again . . . 'I do want it to happen,' she whispered, looking at him. 'I want — '

She broke off, aware of the colour draining from Kyle's face; aware of his body tensing, his eyes darkening, his knuckles turning white as his hands clenched the steering wheel. She looked away from him to follow his intense gaze.

There was a bright red sports car parked on his cottage driveway. Kyle's voice was cold and bitter — freezing her very soul — as he rasped, 'It's Denise. I'll have to go and see what she wants. I'll come over when she's gone.'

He stopped the car and leaned over her to open her door. For a moment, Tiphanie paused; waiting for an apology, a few words of regret maybe? But there was nothing. He didn't even look at her.

She had no option other than getting out of the car. Hobson's Choice, she thought, almost hysterically. And, forcing herself not to run, she made her way slowly towards the bridge.

On this very bridge they'd talked about starting over, about cherishing the feeling between them, allowing it to grow. How could it grow when Denise was still part of his life? Tristan had said Denise was engaged, so what was she doing here? She hadn't been in the car, there'd been no sign of her, so she must be in the cottage, and that meant she had a key. Did Denise still hold the key to Kyle's heart?

Numbly, Tiphanie stared towards the cottage. Kyle was striding up the path towards the front door. She saw it open, caught a glimpse of long, blonde hair. ''Long blonde hair and a face like an angel's.' That's how Tris described her,' she muttered. But Tristan had also said Kyle was probably glad to be shot of her.

Trying to console herself with that thought, Tiphanie hurried to Marsh View. Kyle had said he'd come over when Denise had gone. Tiphanie just hoped that would be soon.

12

Twilight turned to dusk; the dusk turned to darkness. Tiphanie's mind was a crazy mixture of hope and despair. It seemed like a different age when she'd made coffee and sandwiches and carried them up to the studio to wait for Kyle. She'd seen the heron of the night before wing its way home, telling herself that seeing it was a lucky omen, and Kyle would be here soon.

The phone had rung and she'd hurried to answer it, convinced she'd hear Kyle's voice. But it was her father telling her he'd been home for three days and asking why she hadn't been in touch. She'd apologised and told him she'd been busy working. 'I'm still busy,' she'd added, knowing that if he thought she was working he'd get off the phone quickly. True, Kyle had said he'd come over; but Denise's red sports car was still there, so maybe he'd phone instead.

The coffee was cold now, though, and the sandwiches curling disdainfully at the edges; but still Tiphanie sat curled up on the window-seat, straining her eyes towards Kyle's cottage. The lights were on and all the curtains drawn across the windows, shutting her out. She hadn't seen anyone closing the curtains; that must have happened when she'd reluctantly moved and gone down to feed Crystal and Marmaduke.

What if she were to see their shadows on the curtains? Shadows of them entwined together. Wasn't there an old song about that? Yes, there was, but that song told the story of someone looking at the wrong house. He hadn't really seen his love in someone else's arms.

Kyle wasn't her love, though, was he? Tiphanie anguished. He obviously still belongs to Denise. She's been there for hours; they'll spend the night together — the night that should have been mine and Kyle's. But all the time I've known him, which actually wasn't very long, all the time we've spent together has been borrowed, a sort of invitation to take what's not and what can't be really mine.

How could Kyle have talked about trust only to betray her trust like this? He couldn't wait to get rid of her when he saw Denise's car outside his place. Why had he let her think it was all over between him and Denise?

Tiphanie sighed. Kyle had said he wanted to trust her, said Denise had tarnished him. He'd probably given up on his ex-wife because she was engaged to be married to someone else.

'So was he just using me?' she murmured aloud. He had felt something for her. But it was obvious now it had just been a physical attraction. If only her feelings had remained at that and hadn't turned to love. All this would have been easier to bear then. And how long would it take for her love to die? Even if it *ever* died, the memories would remain. Especially this one of sitting in the dark all alone and waiting for something that clearly wasn't going to happen now.

Nevertheless, Tiphanie sat there watching and waiting until all the lights in the cottage had gone out, and even for a while after that, turning on all the lights in Marsh View so that Kyle might see them and know she was awake. Awake and waiting for him.

Eventually, tiredness, coldness and despair drove her to bed. She didn't cry, her hurt went too deep for that. But a couple of old songs by England Dan and John Ford Coley kept playing through her mind. 'Say I love you, say goodbye . . . ' Kyle hadn't said that, but neither had they said goodbye. Perhaps 'Nights are Forever Without You' was more appropriate, because this night seemed to be never-ending.

She must have slept, finally, for she woke with a start and wondered what the noise was. An insistent trilling noise. She hadn't set her alarm clock, had she? No, she hadn't; that had been the last thing on her mind. All her misery surged back, but the trilling continued. Suddenly, she realised it was the phone; she'd never got used to the strange noise Tristan's phone made. Maybe she didn't want to hear it now anyway. It was bringing her back into the real world, and she wasn't sure she wanted to be there.

Sighing wearily she got out of bed, half-hoping the phone would stop ringing before she got there. It didn't, and she picked it up without speaking. Then came the voice she most wanted to hear. *No.* Where had that thought come from? She didn't want to hear Kyle, she wanted to forget about him and pretend he had never happened. But his voice was low and husky, it was tearing at her heart; and, against her will, she listened.

'I'm sorry, Tiphanie, so sorry. Believe me, I couldn't get away, couldn't contact you. I've got an appointment today, I mentioned that on Sunday, remember? But I'll be back tonight. Wait for me, Tiphanie. Please wait for me and I'll explain everything, I promise.'

She still hadn't spoken when he ended the call, hadn't been able to. Hope had spiralled through her on hearing his words, and she was frightened to think that everything was going to be all right after all.

And what now? How was she going to fill the day in while waiting for him? Guiltily, she realised she should do some work, but she knew she wouldn't be able to concentrate on new cartoons or on creating Christmassy stories for her Frolic family. She had roughed out a fair amount for the Story Magazine, though. She could go and show it to her editor. Yes, she'd give Natasha a ring and see if she was free.

She could thank Natasha for drawing her attention to that advert, too. And she could also call in at the suppliers to see if the goods they were offering lived up to expectations. Smiling because she'd worked out how to fill her time usefully, she put the cats out and then went to have a shower.

It was later, after she'd dressed and applied light make-up, and was transferring her mother's wedding band to her own left hand, that she remembered she hadn't properly got round to telling Kyle the reason she sometimes wore the ring on her wedding finger.

'I'll tell him about the managing editor only employing married freelancers tonight,' she said to her reflection. Then realised she was acting as though she believed everything would be all right. And it will be, she told herself as she went up to the studio to contact Natasha. He wouldn't have phoned me otherwise.

Having so far resisted the temptation to look across and see if the red sports car was still parked in Kyle's drive, Tiphanie went to the window. The car was still there. Pulling a face, she turned away, only to catch sight of someone walking across the bridge. 'Long blonde hair, immaculate clothes — and what's more, she's carrying Marmaduke,' Tiphanie groaned.

Glancing down at herself, she felt glad she was wearing a soft green swirly skirt and a pretty floral top, instead of her more usual jeans and tee-shirt. Glad, too, she'd taken time to wash and blow-dry her hair and put make-up on.

Fixing a smile to her face, she went slowly down the winding stairs and, opening the front door, strolled out casually to face the unexpected, unwelcome visitor.

'Your cat, I believe?' Denise laughed, an attractive silvery laugh, and placed a purring Marmaduke into Tiphanie's arms.

Traitor, Tiphanie told her cat silently, as she nodded in response to Denise's question.

'It's a good job Kyle didn't see it — you probably know he can't stand cats? The first thing I'll do when I get back from my honeymoon will be to get a couple. Oh, here's another one — you've got two.' Denise bent gracefully and held out a hand to Crystal who, with obvious delight, allowed herself to be petted.

So she hasn't broken her engagement, thought Tiphanie. She is still getting married. A warm feeling of relief surged through her. Although she'd tried to convince herself that everything was going to be all right between her and Kyle, she hadn't been really sure until now.

And whatever else, Denise really likes cats and they like her, Tiphanie thought wryly. So she can't be all bad. 'Thank you for bringing Marmaduke back. He probably knew I was going out and tried to disappear so I wouldn't shut him inside.'

'Are you going out straight away?' Denise straightened and met Tiphanie's eyes. 'Only I was hoping I could persuade you to let me take a final look around Marsh View. My husband-to-be doesn't approve of me coming here, so this is the last time. Oh, I haven't even introduced myself, have I? I'm Denise, Kyle's ex-wife. We used to live in the old smock mill, so I really would like to say a last goodbye to it.'

'I was going to make myself a coffee before I went out.' Tiphanie felt almost friendly in the light of the news Denise had imparted. 'Come in and have one with me while you're saying your farewells.'

'Do you like living here?' Denise asked a few minutes later as Tiphanie set the percolator going.

'I don't live here. I just came to cat-sit for my brother. Crystal . . . ' Tiphanie waved a hand towards the cat. ' . . . is his cat; and Marmaduke, the one who was trespassing, is mine. I do like both Marsh View and the area, though.'

'Kyle was such an idiot to move out,' said Denise. 'Oh, I can understand his reasoning, feeling that Dee-Dee wouldn't like to live here after he and I had.'

'Dee-Dee?' queried Tiphanie, an impending sense of foreboding creeping over her.

'I don't know how well you know Kyle?' Denise seemed to pause for an answer and Tiphanie muttered something about hardly knowing him at all. 'Then at least you won't have the misfortune of offering a lover's devotion.'

Denise sounded bitter as she continued. 'Dee-Dee was married to a cousin of mine. Jake. Well, third cousin really. That's how Kyle and I first met. He and Jake were best friends. Kyle was in love with Dee-Dee even then, and although I knew I was second-best, I married him. I often wondered if the similarity of my name and hers was one of the reasons Kyle proposed. I often get called Dee for short, so he could get away with it if he called me by her name in one of his moments of passion.

'Kyle and I had only been married a few months when he had a crash on his motorbike. He wasn't too badly hurt, but Jake was riding pillion and he was killed. Dee-Dee was pregnant at the time; she miscarried and something went wrong. She thought she could never have any more babies.'

Tiphanie poured two mugs of coffee, though she didn't think she'd manage to drink hers, and sat down to hear the rest. Her mind was in turmoil; she didn't want to hear more, but she *had* to.

'Anyway — ' Denise smiled wistfully. ' — Kyle and I stayed together for about a year after that, and then I couldn't stand it any more. Dee-Dee was working with him, translating his stories; it tore me apart, knowing Kyle still loved her and that she was free. And, what's more . . . ' Denise took a sip of coffee before continuing. ' . . . Kyle felt responsible for her. To be fair, Dee-Dee didn't play on that; she was still mourning Jake, and besides, she said she'd never marry again knowing she couldn't have babies.

'That made Kyle worse, really, the

thought of Dee-Dee wasting her life. He became impossible to live with. I left him and started divorce proceedings. I knew Kyle would try and persuade Dee-Dee to marry him. She remained adamant; she'd never marry again if she couldn't have children. She had a few operations, but none of them worked. Then . . . '

Denise broke off again to drink some more coffee. 'Then, apparently, she had another operation about a month ago. I happened to see her at the hospital yesterday. I'd gone to visit a sick friend and she'd gone for a check-up. She was over the moon. The specialist had told her he could see no reason now why she shouldn't be able to have children.'

'So you came to give Kyle the good news?' Tiphanie said. Though how on earth she'd managed to speak she didn't know.

'Well, Dee-Dee and I went for a drink and she confided in me. Of course, she knew about my forthcoming marriage, I sent her an invitation to the wedding. She told me how she'd come to love Kyle, but didn't know how to tell him she'd marry him if he still wanted her as his wife. I did the only thing possible. After all, I've found happiness — and when you're happy yourself, you want the same for others, don't you?

'So I bundled her into my car — she doesn't drive — and brought her to Kyle. She's gone with him to London today; he had an appointment with a publisher and couldn't cancel, but they obviously couldn't bear to be apart. It's like a fairy tale with happy endings all round, isn't it?'

Denise smiled and got up from the table. 'Well, thanks for the coffee. I'll let you get on with your day. Don't bother to see me out, I know the way. It's been nice meeting you and the cats.' And before Tiphanie could speak or move, Denise had gone.

She didn't even bother to have a look around, thought Tiphanie. She just walked in here and shattered my life.

Now I know what Kyle was going to explain tonight. He was going to tell me about Dee-Dee. Well, if he thinks I'm going to wait to hear him unburden his soul, he's got another think coming. I'm going home. I'll take Crystal with me, and she'll just have to get used to being in strange surroundings.

Moving slowly, feeling like an old woman, she got up from the table, automatically picking up the coffee mugs and taking them to the sink. Then she noticed the time on the wall clock. She hadn't got time to pack her things, sort out travelling cages for Crystal and Marmaduke, and still keep her appointment with Natasha.

She couldn't cancel, not after arranging to see her only a short while ago. That would be unprofessional — and besides, Tiphanie knew she would need her work more than ever now. She'd bury herself in it. It was the only thing she had left. She'd have to come back to pack, and there'd still be time to get away before Kyle returned tonight.

It was as though she were an automaton; she had no recall of leaving Marsh View and getting in her car to drive to Peterborough. It was only when her car phone rang that she fully realised where she was.

'Tiphanie — ' It was her father. ' — I need to see you urgently, pet. I tried phoning Tristan's but you weren't there. So guessing you might be in the car on your way to somewhere . . . I didn't want to phone you on your mobile. I hope you're on hands-free.'

'I am. And you'll see me tonight. I'm coming home.'

'Any chance of seeing you before tonight? Where are you going now?'

'To the publishers in Peterborough. I'll come and see you when I've finished there,' she told him, not really caring where she went after seeing Natasha or why she was going. Normally, she might have wondered at the urgency. It wasn't like her father to be impatient.

★ ★ ★

'You don't look like your normal bubbly self, Tiphanie,' said Natasha. 'You walked over to my desk as though you were a puppet having its strings pulled.'

'I've been burning the candle at both ends,' Tiphanie replied, knowing Natasha would think she meant that was because she'd been working.

'OK, let's have a look at what you've been doing, then.'

Tiphanie even managed to force a smile as Natasha declared the roughs were brilliant and already had the spark of magic she knew Tiphanie was capable of.

'Did you look at that advert I left you a note about?' Natasha asked as she laughed at Tiphanie's cartoon to go with the waxworks story.

'Yes, and I'm going to call in at the suppliers when I leave here and get one.'

'No need to do that,' Natasha said. 'The manufacturers sent some samples. They're in the warehouse. Choose whichever one you want on your way out. Contributor's perk,' she added, smiling.

'Thanks, that's great. It will save me time not going to their workshop. Have you got the rest of the stories for the new magazine yet?'

'No, but I've approved the synopses, and the stories should be here by tomorrow. You don't fancy working in-house for a couple of days, do you? It might save a bit of time if you work alongside the graphic designers. That's if you can make arrangements for someone to pick the twins up,' she added loudly, and Tiphanie guessed the managing editor was close by.

'I'm sure their grandma will have them,' Tiphanie replied truthfully. 'And now I'd better be going.'

'You can drive round to the loading bay and choose your sample,' Natasha said by way of farewell.

'Thanks, I'll do that. And I'll see you tomorrow.'

* ★ ★

Tiphanie's father was in the garden when she drew up outside the house. His step was sprightly and almost boyish as he hurried down the path, and as she got out of the car, Tiphanie thought he looked as if he'd shed years.

'I was hoping you'd be on your own,' he said, looking over her shoulder as he hugged her.

'Come and meet Harry. It's OK, Dad, he won't want to come in.'

'He's . . . He's . . . ' Her father stuttered as he peered closely at Harry sitting in the passenger seat.

'Yes, Harry — that's the name the suppliers gave him, and it suits him, so I'm calling him that — is made of a sort of rubbery plastic stuff.' Tiphanie chuckled. 'He's my personal bodyguard. A dummy escort. He looks real if you don't get too close, doesn't he? A real hunk of a man — or should I say mannequin?' Then she sobered.

'It's a marvellous idea for women travelling alone in a car. They're going to be advertised in a magazine I'm working on. I got him for free, courtesy of the publishers.'

'I'll feel happier about you driving alone now. Especially as Tristan's place is so far off the beaten track. The twins phoned last night and told me all about it.'

'Yes, but like I told you when you phoned me, I'm coming home tonight, Dad.'

'What about Tristan's cat? I spoke to him yesterday and he said he won't be back for a few days yet.'

'I'll bring Crystal with me. You seem to have a remarkable grip on things, Dad. You're usually a bit absent-minded.'

'My trip to Carrickfergus was extremely fruitful. King John spent a lot of time there and I met someone who knows all there is to know about that period. We talked about the tract we're writing, and in fact we're going to embark on a new-look history series together.

'That's the problem, Tiphanie.' Following him into the kitchen, she tried to pretend an interest in the new décor. 'This friend is coming to stay.'

'So why's that a problem?'

'I could do with borrowing your bedroom. The decorators found dry rot in the two spare bedrooms. Madge contacted me and I agreed we should get it sorted straight away. The floorboards have been ripped out so the rooms are unusable. Your room is fine, though, and I thought you wouldn't be here,' he added almost pleadingly.

'Couldn't the professor stay in a hotel? There are plenty of good ones nearby.'

'It isn't the professor, and . . . and my guest is a she. I'd love you to come and meet her, though.'

There he goes, taking me for granted again, thought Tiphanie. But she couldn't summon up the energy to protest. Nothing seemed to matter as much as what Kyle had put her through. Now she'd been forced into staying at Marsh View, she'd have to work out a way of avoiding him. Though maybe . . .

'If you want to yell and shout, get on and do it!' her father bawled. 'I can't stand silent anger, Tiphanie.'

'I'm not angry at you, Dad. Well, not too angry. I was thinking of something else. Go ahead and let your friend use my room; and if you want me to meet her, you can take us for a meal. Somewhere expensive and impressive,' she added teasingly. Even though she was suffering heartache, she wasn't selfish enough to spoil her father's newfound happiness.

'I've already booked a table at the Swan for eight-thirty on Thursday,' he said, smiling.

'Great. I'll look forward to that. But I'll be off now, Dad. I need to sort out a few things because I'm working in-house at the publishers for the next couple of days.'

And at least it will only be early mornings and evenings when I have to avoid Kyle, she realised as she walked towards the kitchen door.

★ ★ ★

Cat food was one thing Tiphanie needed to sort out, so she decided to call in at the mini-market on the main road before the turn off that led to Tristan's.

Just as she was going into the shop, she met Denise coming out. 'I'm on my way home,' Denise said. 'I called in here to get some postcards of the area. Part of my last farewell, really. If you see Kyle, could you pass on a message? Oh, but . . . ' She was glancing towards Tiphanie's parked car. 'I see you've got a friend with you. He looks a bit of all right. Passing on a message is probably the last thing you'll want to think about. And I'll be phoning Kyle later on, anyway.'

Delighted that the dummy escort had

more than passed muster with Denise, Tiphanie thought quickly. 'Yes,' she said. 'Harry and I split up some time back, but when we met today we both realised how much we'd missed each other. He'll be staying with me at Marsh View for a while. A sort of trial run to see if we can live together.'

She hoped that information would be passed on to Kyle when Denise phoned him. Because it would be the perfect way to stop Kyle from calling. She'd sit Harry in the lounge window. Maybe sit next to him and manoeuvre one of his arms around her. There'd be no way Kyle would want to come and 'explain everything' knowing she wasn't alone. Though she hoped Kyle wouldn't be around when she had to carry Harry from or to her car.

★   ★   ★

Later, after managing to get Harry inside unseen by anyone other than the cats, Tiphanie sat him on the lounge window seat and then, after feeding Crystal and Marmaduke, went to get changed into something slinky and sexy. If she was going to sit next to Harry — posing in case Kyle looked over — she wanted to look the part.

She felt slightly ridiculous as she walked into the lounge and thought about sitting next to Harry. It was different when she was using him in his rightful capacity; having him in the passenger seat of her car gave her a sense of security, and she blessed the unknown person who'd come up with the idea. But using him in this way . . .

Shrugging, she poured herself a brandy for courage, and then went over to the window seat. She grimaced slightly as she manoeuvred one of Harry's arms into place around her shoulders, and then for the second evening running she sat watching Kyle's cottage.

Her emotional day, the effort of not giving in to her feelings in front of anyone, and the brandy, must have all combined to send her to sleep because she came to with a start when she heard a hammering at the front door.

It wasn't dark yet, only slightly dusky, so if it was Kyle, he'd have seen Harry through the window. Heart thudding, she stumbled over to open the door.

Kyle stood there, his emanating rage a tangible property. He thrust a bundle of letters at her. 'Tristan's mail. I collected it this morning. I see, for once, my ex-wife was telling the truth,' he rasped. 'You've brought someone back with you. My first impressions of you having numerous men friends were right after all.'

'What if I have? You've no right to dictate what I do, who I see, and it's nothing to do with you if I want to spend the night with one of them. Except Harry is special. When we met unexpectedly today, I realised he'd always be the only man who could ever mean anything to me.'

She felt surprised when Kyle's eyes clouded over with what looked like genuine pain and regret, and how his Adam's apple jerked as though he were fighting for control. But why should he feel hurt? He was back with Dee-Dee, the only one who could ever mean anything to *him*. Maybe he was just regretting the fact he hadn't managed to explain that? Whatever, Tiphanie knew she'd never forget the look on his face before he turned, went down the steps, and walked away.

13

'Have you heard of Jonas Jeffries, Tiphanie?' It was Tiphanie's second day of working in-house when Natasha asked the question.

'He writes sci-fi of some sort,' Tiphanie replied. 'The twins love his books. I've never read any, though.'

'They're brilliant,' said Natasha. 'They're spoof sci-fi and extremely funny. Apparently the author is shy and secretive, so the project is being handled through his agent.'

'What project?' Tiphanie could tell Natasha was excited about something.

'Hopefully, we'll get the go-ahead for us to adapt some of his stories into a comic strip. You're the obvious choice for the artwork; and we've a writer who, some time ago, submitted a few sci-fi manuscripts. They were good, but didn't fit with our publishing plans at the time. But we think he'd be the one to adapt the stories. Come and meet him. Angus is off today, so I've borrowed his office: there'll be more privacy there.'

Grabbing her large canvas bag, Tiphanie followed Natasha. Her steps faltered when she walked through the door and she stared at the arm and hand resting on the low shelving at the side of Angus's desk. Head and body were hidden from view, but Tiphanie didn't need to see any more. She'd have known, even without the glint of the heavy gold chain on the wrist, that it was Kyle.

Fate could be so darned cruel at times, she thought, as Natasha started to introduce them.

'We've met before. How are you, Tiphanie?' Kyle's tone was grim, his eyes cold and mocking.

Murmuring something, Tiphanie sat down before her legs gave way. But through her shock, she wondered if Kyle had seen Harry this morning

— she'd left him sitting in the lounge window. Travelling to and from Peterborough during rush hour and in broad daylight, she hadn't felt in need of her 'bodyguard'.

'Right,' Natasha said briskly, 'I've another meeting soon, but it won't be a long one. I've a photocopy of one of the stories we're thinking of adapting for both of you. I thought while I'm gone you could read through it and talk over any ideas you might get.'

She handed each of them a set of photocopies. 'I've yet another meeting after lunch, and that one could last all afternoon. I don't suppose you're both free tonight, are you? We could go for a meal and work out how to handle things. Then, if you could both come in for the whole day tomorrow as well, we can — '

'Sorry, it'll have to be just tomorrow for me,' interrupted Tiphanie. 'I'm not free tonight. I've got a special date.' That was for Kyle's benefit, but meeting her father and his new friend was a special occasion.

'Just tomorrow for me as well,' Kyle said. 'I've an appointment with a vicar this evening.'

Tiphanie bit back a gasp. Kyle and Dee-Dee must be planning to marry soon if he was seeing the vicar tonight. A sensation of desolation crept over her and she looked at Natasha. 'I'm sorry, Natasha, you'll have to find someone else. I can't do this, can't work with . . . ' She glanced across at Kyle.

'Oh, I'm sure we could work together, Tiphanie,' Kyle drawled.

'If you think I could keep meeting you to discuss the stories and act as though nothing has ever happened between us . . . ' Remembering where she was and Natasha's presence, Tiphanie buried her face in her hands. 'I'm sorry, Natasha, I just can't do it.'

'Look, I've got to get to my meeting,' said Natasha. 'Maybe you two could talk things over while I'm gone. Try and get her to change her mind, Kyle,' she added. And Tiphanie heard Natasha get up and leave the office.

Strong but gentle fingers coaxed Tiphanie's hands down from her face, and then with a delicate butterfly touch, wiped her tears away.

*   *   *

She looked so vulnerable, so appealing. Kyle wanted to hold her close, love her, cherish her and soothe all the hurting away — hers and his own. Seeing her like this was tearing him apart; he could almost forget what she'd done to him, almost forgive her for her betrayal.

With immense effort, he pulled himself together. There was no way he'd enter a fool's paradise again. He stood up, thrusting his hands in his pockets so he wouldn't be tempted to touch her. 'We can't let personal feelings get in the way of our careers, Tiphanie. Besides, you've managed to act in rather more than a friendly manner towards me several times. You really had me fooled, so I wouldn't have thought you'd have much trouble in letting Natasha think we get on well enough to work together. You'd just have to act out another lie.'

★   ★   ★

I've been acting out lies ever since I first met him, Tiphanie thought painfully. Then again, he did the same by pretending our friendship could grow into something else, when all the time he was in love with Dee-Dee.

'OK,' she said. 'You've made a couple of good points, there, Kyle, so let's read this story and see if either of us get a eureka moment.' She doubted he'd ever know how hard it had been to say that.

She forced herself to concentrate and, in spite of everything, her professional side began to take over. Natasha had said the stories were extremely funny, and this one certainly was. She could already see some of the characters and their weird space machines in her mind's eye. She rootled in her bag for paper and a pencil and began sketching.

'Well, you certainly had a eureka moment, Tiphanie.' Kyle had come to stand behind her and was looking over her shoulder. 'These are the other side of brilliant. I just hope my words will be worthy of your drawings.'

'I'm sure they will.' Natasha had come back in time to hear his words. 'Is everything all right, Tiphanie?' she added.

'Yes, fine,' Tiphanie said, managing to sound as if she meant it. 'Sorry about before, Natasha. I guess I'm over-tired. And, as Kyle pointed out to me, there's no way personal feelings should interfere with our work.'

'I'm glad to hear that. I'm sure with you two on board we'll get the go-ahead, and a sci-fi magazine could be a biggie for us. I'd like to try for translation rights as well.'

'Kyle might come in useful there,' Tiphanie said. Her heart shattered even more as she added, 'Dee-Dee, his wife-to-be, is a translator; isn't she, Kyle?'

'That's good to know,' Natasha said into the silence that had fallen. 'But why don't you go home now, Tiphanie? You'll have all afternoon to get ready for your special date. You got a lot done yesterday, and we're right on schedule so far with plans for the Story Magazine and your own Christmas Special. So we can spend all day tomorrow discussing the newest project.'

'Right. Good idea. I'll see you both tomorrow, then.' And I'll need to put on a really good act so Kyle can't guess how much I'm hurting inside, she thought as she put the photocopied story, her rough sketches, and her pencil in her bag before hurrying away.

* * *

Tiphanie had only made it half-way across the car park before Kyle caught up with her and grabbed hold of one arm. 'We're going for a drive in my car,' he said. 'And don't throw a tantrum, Tiphanie. We've got things to discuss.'

She was about to struggle until he added, 'Mainly, how you thought I could possibly be marrying Dee-Dee when . . . when . . . ' He broke off and then continued, 'I don't even know who mentioned her to you. Probably the twins after they'd been to my place and saw my dedication to her in one of the books she'd translated. But they couldn't have thought I was about to marry her.'

'They didn't mention her. It was your ex-wife.'

'Denise spoke to you? Look, we can't talk here. Please come for a drive, Tiphanie.'

★ ★ ★

After a short but silent journey, Kyle parked in a quiet country lane. 'So, exactly what did Denise say about Dee-Dee, Tiphanie?'

'That she could now have babies and

could also admit she loved you and would marry you as you wanted.' Tiphanie was crying now, but managed to tell Kyle everything else about his ex-wife's visit.

'I've never been in love with Dee-Dee. I thought I loved Denise and that she returned my feelings. Soon after our marriage, she told me she'd always been in love with Jake and had married me so Dee-Dee wouldn't suspect anything. She told me she was going to do her best to split Jake and Dee-Dee up because Jake loved her and not Dee-Dee, and that she and Jake were sleeping together.'

'Was it true?'

Kyle shook his head. 'I couldn't believe it of my best friend, but I asked him about it. He was never unfaithful to Dee-Dee, and although Denise had several times made a play for him, he couldn't stand her. And that's putting it politely. Denise never forgave me for checking her lies with Jake, or for me telling her what Jake thought of her.'

'But why would Denise tell *me* so many lies?' Tiphanie asked.

'To take her revenge on me, I guess. You see, that day you and I returned from Cambridge, Denise *had* brought Dee-Dee to see me, and I spent half the night convincing her that Jake would want her to marry again. Not marry *me*, but a man called Andy, whom she's known over a year now. Dee-Dee and I have only ever been friends. Her father is dead and I'll be giving her away. That's why I'm going to see the vicar with her and Andy this evening.'

'That doesn't explain why Denise lied to me to get revenge on you, Kyle.'

'I spent the other half of the night refusing to sell Denise Marsh View. Apparently, she'd told her fiancé the old smock mill was hers. I told *her* that as soon as Tristan's lease ran out, I was planning to move back in — told her I was hoping to marry someone special, kind, gentle and adorable who, I knew would help me overcome my fear of heights vertigo as well.

'I don't know how she knew I meant you. I suppose she overheard me telling Dee-Dee about you. And to Denise's mind it was you standing in the way of me selling her Marsh View, so by telling all those lies, she'll have hoped you'd disappear out of my life and I wouldn't want to move into Marsh View without you. And I wouldn't have wanted to.

'But of course, it's all immaterial now because at that time, I didn't know you were about to get back with the only man you could ever love.'

Joy filled Tiphanie's heart and she began to laugh through her tears. 'Harry isn't real; he's a dummy escort to sit in the passenger seat as a bodyguard for when I'm driving alone at night. Denise saw him in my car from the doorway of the mini-market. I made up that story about him, hoping she'd tell you. She'd said she'd be phoning you that evening . . . and I was heartbroken, Kyle, because I thought you were marrying Dee-Dee. I wanted to let you think you'd never really meant anything to me. And I carried him indoors and sat him in the lounge window and sat next to him, hoping you might see us and think . . . '

'Stop burbling, Tiphanie and let me kiss you.'

Crushing her to him, he kissed the tip of her nose and then her eyes and finally he reached her mouth. It was a kiss for her tired soul to melt into and she wanted it to last forever. But he broke it off with a groan.

'It's rather uncomfortable kissing you in the front of a car,' he said, smiling tenderly.

'And there's still something I haven't explained,' she said a bit breathlessly. And she went on to tell him exactly why she wore her mother's wedding band on her own wedding finger when she visited the publishers.

'Very soon, this managing editor could be employing you as a married freelancer,' Kyle said huskily. 'And you'll be wearing a ring on your wedding finger for love, not to earn money.'

'I . . . I . . . Are you . . . ' Did she dare hope this was Kyle's way of proposing to her?

'You will marry me, won't you?' he asked anxiously. 'I know we haven't really known each other long but I feel as if we've known each other all our lives. Through bad times and good,' he added wryly.

'Well,' Tiphanie pretended to think. 'The twins would be delighted. Zoe is already half in love with you. I suspect my father has a few ideas of his own about remarrying, so he'd be glad to get rid of me. Oh, and my date tonight is with him and his lady friend. But . . . '

'But what?' Kyle demanded. 'Don't torment me, Tiphanie.'

'What about Marmaduke? You don't like cats.'

'I didn't used to, but I'm crazy about them now. Cats made me realise how much I cared for you that day when I saw you climbing down the tree clutching Tristan's. I was terrified you'd fall. I knew then I loved you. Only . . . '

'Only you thought I was having affairs with a dozen different men, and I let you go on thinking it. Oh, Kyle, just think how close we came to losing each other.'

'You still haven't answered my question,' he said. 'Will you marry me, Tiphanie?'

'You've got to answer a question first. Will you build me a tree-house for a wedding present?' she asked, leaning over to nibble his ear.

And Kyle seemed to forget how uncomfortable he found it, making love in the front seats of his car.

* * *

'You never did answer me properly,' Kyle reminded her quite some time later. 'Will you marry me, Tiphanie?'

'I will,' she replied. Because she knew this time she really had found the beginning of the rest of her life.

We do hope that you have enjoyed reading this large print book.

Did you know that all of our titles are available for purchase?

We publish a wide range of high quality large print books including:
Romances, Mysteries, Classics
General Fiction
Non Fiction and Westerns

Special interest titles available in large print are:
The Little Oxford Dictionary
Music Book, Song Book
Hymn Book, Service Book

Also available from us courtesy of Oxford University Press:
Young Readers' Dictionary
(large print edition)
Young Readers' Thesaurus
(large print edition)

For further information or a free brochure, please contact us at:
Ulverscroft Large Print Books Ltd.,
The Green, Bradgate Road, Anstey,
Leicester, LE7 7FU, England.
Tel: (00 44) **0116 236 4325**
Fax: (00 44) **0116 234 0205**

LOVE WILL FIND A WAY

Miranda Barnes

Convalescing after a car accident, Gwen Yorke leases a remote cottage on the beautiful Isle of Skye. She hopes to find inspiration there for her career as a rug designer, and wants to decide if she and her boyfriend have a future together. In Glenbrittle, she finds herself drawn to the enigmatic, moody Andrew McIver, and his young daughter Fiona. To Gwen's delight, she and Fiona become close, frequently sketching together. But why is Andrew so unhappy about their friendship?

THE PRINCE'S BRIDE

Sophie Weston

One of three royal brothers in the Adriatic principality of San Michele, Prince Jonas works hard. But after a protocol-ridden evening, he's due some downtime in his beloved forest. Hope Kennard was the daughter of the manor back in England. But she has guarded her heart since her childhood ended in financial scandal. She's just passing through San Michele, before moving on to another country, another job. But then a charming forest ranger appears. And this time, her instincts don't help . . .